SUNFLOWER SERENADE

SUNFLOWER SERENADE

Tricia Goyer

Guideposts

NEW YORK, NEW YORK

To my sister Melissa, who sings like an angel.
Don't give up on your dreams.

And to my daughter Leslie—
keep writing songs and using your talents for God!

Acknowledgments

There are so many people in my life who do so much. Because of them, my heart is glad.

There are those living with me (John, Cory, Leslie, Nathan, Grandma Dolores and Andrea) and those in my life (church friends, community friends, writer friends, online friends). Thank you.

I always thank Janet Kobobel Grant because she's the most amazing agent ever and my assistant Amy Lathrop because she manages my writing life. Yeah! I also always thank my mom, dad and other family members because they love me, even under deadline.

Yet for this book there are quite a few people who deserve much credit. Thank you to Beth Adams and Fiona Serpa, two great editors. Also thank you to the great people who helped me with favorite memories and/or information about the county fair: Max Elliot Anderson, Lorna Seilstad, Jane Wells, Anne McDonald, Gayle Gresham, Danielle McIntosh and Tara Norick. Colleen Shine and producer Eric Welch were very accommodating with information on making music videos, and Gary Van Riper and Roy Polmanteer (Twitter friends) lent a hand with song titles. Thanks to Wanda Rosseland for general help about life on a farm!

Finally, thank you to my daughter Leslie who assisted me with the music and lyrics for the song "Sunflower Serenade." I started with an idea, and you made music!

—Tricia Goyer

Home to Heather Creek

Before the Dawn

Sweet September

Circle of Grace

Homespun Harvest

A Patchwork Christmas

An Abundance of Blessings

Every Sunrise

Promise of Spring

April's Hope

Seeds of Faith

On the Right Path

Sunflower Serenade

SUNFLOWER SERENADE

Chapter One

Charlotte rolled down the car window and let the warm air swirl in, imagining the scent of cotton candy, fair burgers, and barbecue. She smiled as she noticed the large semitrailer driving ahead of her, illustrated with colorful clowns and the words FUN HOUSE painted on its side. The rides were arriving, which meant the horse trailers and family campers soon would follow.

"Fun house—they should come to our house, right, Christopher?" She clicked on her left turn signal and turned onto Lincoln Street.

"Yeah, it's a little crazy. I didn't know the fair would make the town like this." Christopher twirled his finger next to the side of his head.

"It's like this every year, and we're especially busy getting projects ready to be entered, helping the church set up its pie booth, attending the rodeo and pig-wrestling events . . . and, of course, serving on the fair board."

"The fair board? What's that?"

"The fair board is the group that organizes what's happening at the fair and decides what entertainers to bring in each year."

1

Christopher gasped from the passenger's seat, and Charlotte glanced over at him.

"You decided that?" Christopher scratched his blond head and wrinkled his nose.

Charlotte laughed. "Well, I wasn't the only one who decided on that, but I did vote that it was a good idea. Everyone says Shae Lynne is a popular, new singer, although I really haven't kept up with those things."

A family, all dressed in jeans, boots, and cowboy hats, paused at the sidewalk, and Charlotte stopped the car and let them cross the street in front of her, offering a friendly wave. She was on her way to Rosemary's house to drop off the pies she'd promised to make and donate for the church's fair booth. Rosemary had an extra freezer where the pies would be safe until fair time. Keeping them at home, Charlotte knew, would be far from safe. Not only was there no extra room in their freezer, but any pie in their house was considered "open game" to any of the kids—or worse, to Bob, who didn't need the sugar. More than that, taking them into town now got another item checked off Charlotte's to-do list. The idea of baking and taking fresh pies to the fair on Monday would be impossible with so much else going on.

Up and down Lincoln Street, every window was plastered with posters advertising the fair—although, truth be told, it really didn't need much advertisement. No visitor could walk around Bedford for ten minutes without knowing what was up. For many, the fair was the highlight of the summer. Every conversation centered around it, and for some, life changed for the week. Many livestock families even camped at the fairgrounds during fair week to take care of their animals.

"Look!" Christopher pointed to another truck four cars ahead. "That's pieces of the Squirrel Cages. I love that ride!"

"You do? Is that the one that spins you around and flips you upside down?"

"Yeah, it's awesome. When I rode it at a school carnival in San Diego a girl in the car in front of me puked all over everyone. Tons of kids got sick, but not me, even when a chunk—"

"Okay, Christopher," Charlotte interrupted. "That's quite enough, thank you."

A wide grin filled Christopher's face, and Charlotte turned her mind to happier thoughts. She imagined the rows of RVs parked in the camping area of the county fair, seeing old friends, catching up with people who had moved away from Bedford but who still made it back every August to enjoy good wholesome fun.

The warm summer sun shone through the car windows, and Charlotte realized that, to her, "fair days" were as familiar as swimming in the creek, eating watermelon on the front porch, and going for long walks in the twilight down country roads.

"Oh, look, there's Hannah." Charlotte spotted her friend walking into Fabrics and Fun and waved. "I wonder if she's—"

"Grandma, stop!" Christopher's shout split the air, and Charlotte glanced toward the roadside just in time to see a lamb, of all things, darting right in front of her. She slammed on the brakes and the car stopped inches away from the lamb. She felt herself flying forward against her seatbelt. Next to her, Christopher's body jerked forward and his hand hit the dashboard.

The lamb stopped in fear, and then darted back the way it had come, scurrying down the sidewalk and weaving through the people who watched in surprise.

The sound of Charlotte's pies tumbling across the back-seat made her cringe. She had been in a hurry and hadn't bothered getting out the pie holder that Pete had made for her. Now she hated to turn around and look.

Charlotte glanced around her, trying to figure out where the lamb had come from, and noticed a boy on the side-walk. He gazed at Charlotte with wide eyes. In his hand was a long stick he most likely used to guide his lamb.

Charlotte sighed. She knew that during the month before the fair 4-H members practiced leading their lambs and setting them up for competition, but whatever had possessed him to practice on the main street in town with so many cars around?

She placed a hand over her pounding heart, and had barely caught her breath when Christopher opened the door and jumped from the car.

"Grandma, that's David's lamb. I better help him catch it."

Christopher slammed the door and was already hurrying toward the sidewalk before she had a chance to warn him not to run out into the road. She didn't want another close call on these busy streets.

Charlotte inched her car to the side and then double-parked next to an older sedan so she could get a quick view of the damage.

Please let the mess not be as bad as it sounded. She turned and peered into the backseat.

It was worse.

One apple pie was facedown on her back floorboard. The other pies had stayed in the cardboard boxes she'd used to carry them, but they'd flipped onto their sides and gotten smashed as the boxes had flown forward.

Charlotte let out a deep sigh and looked up just in time to see that an older man had snagged the lamb and was helping Christopher get a rope around its neck. Once the lamb was on its leash, the other boy, David, walked shyly with Christopher back to her car. The lamb trailed behind, confused by what had happened.

"Sorry, Mrs. Stevenson," David said, stepping toward the car. Charlotte noticed he held the rope with an iron grip. "I was walking Bluebell, practicing for the lamb showmanship competition, and she ran away."

Charlotte cocked an eyebrow. "Okay, but you better get that lamb home before something else like this happens." She patted David's shoulder. "You're just lucky little Bluebell wasn't smashed by the Squirrel Cages."

Charlotte paused, amused by her own words. Now that wasn't something she said every day.

"Grandma!" Charlotte turned as Emily's voice split the air. She looked in the direction of Mel's Place and spotted Emily heading her way. Her granddaughter had spent the night with Ashley so the two girls could help out at Mel's Place during the busy pre-fair days.

"Ashley and I were outside washing the windows and we saw everything that happened. Are you okay?"

Charlotte gave Emily a quick hug. "Yeah, I'm fine, but I can't say the same thing about the pies I was taking to Rosemary's."

Emily glanced in the backseat. "Oh, what a mess." Then she flipped her hair over her shoulder, and Charlotte knew her thoughts weren't on the pies at all. "Can I go with you?"

"With me?"

"To Aunt Rosemary's house."

Charlotte motioned for another car to pass by. "Well, now I don't really need to go there."

"Because Rosemary saw me helping at Mel's Place this morning and she said to come with you. She says she has something for me." Emily clapped her hands together.

"Well, I guess I can still swing by, but we can't stay long. Looks like I need to head home and do some more baking."

Emily ran back to Mel's Place to grab her bag and returned to the car. She moved the front seat forward so she could climb into the back. She found a place on the seat that wasn't a mess; then she helped readjust the boxes.

She stuck her finger into one of the pies and scooped out a large strawberry.

"At least it still tastes good," she mumbled as she plopped the syrupy strawberry into her mouth. "How much you want to bet the guys won't even care that they're smooshed?"

So much for keeping the pies safe, Charlotte thought, *and for keeping Bob away from sugar. So much for trying to keep ahead of the game this week.*

Chapter Two

O h, no!" Christopher's eyes widened. "What a mess," he said as he climbed into the front seat.

"You've got that right." Emily said with a mouthful of crumbled pie crust.

"You shouldn't eat those, Emily. Grandma made them for the fair." Then, as if realizing how bad off the pies were, he glanced at Charlotte. "Can they sell smashed pies at the fair?" He wrinkled his nose.

"I don't think so, Christopher." Charlotte looked over her shoulder and noticed a line of cars already growing behind where she was double-parked.

"It is a mess, but we can't sit here and worry about that now. Emily needs to stop by Rosemary's really quick, and then we need to head home and clean this up."

"I know how to clean it up." Christopher waved to David as they drove away.

"You do, do you?" Charlotte eyed him.

"Yeah, just let Toby in here. She loves pie."

Amused by Christopher's comment, Charlotte felt the tension in her shoulders loosen.

"I won't ask how you know Toby likes pie, but I don't think that's a good idea. Too much sugar would probably make her sick, and we need her in tip-top shape for the fair. You've been working too hard on all those tricks to have her get sick now."

"Yeah, you're right." He pointed a finger into the air. "Then I have an idea. We can have Sam, Grandpa, and Uncle Pete eat all the smashed ones."

"There you go," Charlotte chuckled. "I don't think there will be any complaints there."

For a second Charlotte considered if there was a way to hide the smashed pies in the back of the fair booth and just cut slices out of them, but then she considered what the others would think and wrinkled her nose. No, it was probably better just to make new ones to replace them.

Charlotte drove to Rosemary's house, pulling into the alley in back. She parked, and then opened the hatchback. Rosemary must have heard Charlotte's car because she exited the back door of her Cape Cod cottage wearing a Fabrics and Fun apron and a warm smile. She took her glasses from the tip of her nose and allowed them to hang from the chain on her neck. Rosemary's measuring tape also hung around her neck—it was a regular part of her wardrobe. In fact Charlotte was certain the only time she saw Bob's sister without her tape measure was at church. Rosemary brushed a strand of steel-gray hair back from her face as she approached.

"You sewing?" Charlotte's body felt heavy as she climbed out of the car.

"Of course. Isn't it that time of year? I took the day off

from the shop to finish up a few items for the fair, although I'm not getting very far. I've already gotten at least a dozen calls from the girl who's watching the shop for me. It seems everyone around Bedford is up to the same thing, trying to finish one more project. Good ol' Nebraska friendly competition. But enough of that. Let me help."

Rosemary peered into the hatchback. "Oh my!"

"You can say that again." Charlotte sighed.

Christopher jumped from the front seat. Emily got out of the car too.

"My friend David's lamb ran right in front of our car, and Grandma slammed on the brakes."

"Did you miss the lamb?" Rosemary's worried gaze scanned Charlotte's face.

"Thankfully, yes."

"Was it out by the farm?

"No, on Lincoln Street, of all places!"

"Yeah, but some guy helped catch it. I helped too." Christopher's voice rose with excitement. "The lamb almost got run over by the Squirrel Cages."

Rosemary chuckled. "So I guess you won't need to use the freezer?"

"Not today, but maybe tomorrow." Charlotte tried not to sound as weary as she felt. "I know what I'll be doing tonight. Making pies."

"I wish I could help. Maybe I can make one or two." Rosemary's voice was soothing, like a warm cup of tea on a winter's morning.

"No, it's okay. You have enough to do. Maybe the kids will help with the production, just like old times. I'm sure

Emily and Christopher won't mind pitching in. If I start as soon as I get home—"

"Isn't there a fair board meeting after lunch?" Rosemary interrupted.

Charlotte rubbed her temples. "You had to remind me about that, didn't you?"

"Yes, I'm sorry. The only reason I know is because Harriet Walker was in the store yesterday telling me about how much she appreciates you and Bob being back on the board. She says things weren't the same last year without you. Harriet also asked what pie you're entering in the fair. Maybe the pumpkin cloud? That was Jerome's favorite," she said, a wistful look crossing her face as she remembered her late husband.

"Actually, I was thinking of a simple apple-caramel pie. It's easy; I could make one in my sleep." Charlotte sighed. "But that's yet another pie to add to the list."

Rosemary patted Charlotte's shoulder. "Well, that one is my favorite, so it's a good choice."

Rosemary glanced at Emily, and her eyes widened as if she realized the other reason for the visit.

"Oh yes. Emily, I have something for you. It's in the garage."

Charlotte and Emily followed Rosemary into the garage. Charlotte glanced around, appreciating Rosemary's many stored treasures. Rosemary was always in the middle of turning some type of yard sale find into an heirloom. In one corner Charlotte noticed a child-size table and chairs. The set was wooden, and it looked at least forty years old. The paint was chipped and one leg was crooked, causing it to lean. Charlotte's chest constricted as she remembered Denise having a similar one in kindergarten. She wondered what had happened to that old thing. Charlotte's eyes felt moist, and she chided herself for being so sentimental. She didn't have time for this. She had a list of things to take care of before the fair, and now she would be adding pie-baking to that list.

"I found the table at a yard sale," Rosemary said, even before Charlotte asked. "I thought I'd refinish it and save it for Bill and Anna's little one."

Charlotte trailed her fingers over the small table. "I'm sure it will be beautiful after you refinish it, Rosemary. They'll love it. You always give the most thoughtful gifts."

"Speaking of gifts." Rosemary turned to a large camera bag sitting by the back door of the garage. "I put this out here so I wouldn't forget." Rosemary opened the bag, and Charlotte noticed a camera. It was old, but she could tell it had been well cared for.

"A camera?"` A gasp escaped Emily's lips.

"Yes, it belonged to Jerome. He just loved it. We have so many photos he took of his nieces and nephews on our vacations. There are some cute ones of your kids, Charlotte—Bill, Pete . . . Denise." Rosemary's voice grew wobbly.

"Are you sure you want to get rid of it?" Charlotte asked. "I know it means a lot to you."

"Does it even work?" Emily asked, somewhat untactfully.

"Yes it does, Emily." Rosemary assured her. "I know you were saving for a digital camera, but this old-fashioned film kind takes really great photos."

Emily took the camera from the case and skeptically turned it over in her hands.

"I know it looks complicated, but I'm sure you'll get the hang of it," Rosemary encouraged.

"Are you sure?" Charlotte repeated.

"I'm not using it, Charlotte. And it seems right that it should stay in the family. Besides, Emily has an artistic eye. I noticed her taking photos with her cell phone the other day at the shop. I was going to save it until Christmas, but I thought she could use it this week—you know how fun and colorful the fair is. And busy! There will be plenty of things, people, and animals to take photos of."

"Thanks, Aunt Rosemary. I guess I can give it a try." Emily returned the camera to its case and then wrapped her arms around her great-aunt's shoulders.

"You're welcome, dear. There's a manual inside to tell you how everything works. And I'm sure Pete can help too. If I remember correctly, he used to enter some of his pictures in the fair."

Emily nodded and then hurried outside to show Christopher her camera.

Charlotte wished she had as much energy and zeal. "Well, off to make some more pies. You can bet this time I won't be too lazy to transport them in the proper holder. At least if I get them baked today I can scratch that project off the list."

Rosemary squeezed Charlotte's shoulder. "Remember, Char, what needs to get done will. And the rest . . . well, it's not that important."

"I'll try to remember that." She offered Rosemary a slight smile. "Really, I will."

TOBY'S EXCITED BARKING and wagging tail greeted Charlotte and the kids as she parked the car next to the farmhouse. Bob and Pete were leaning under the opened hood of Bob's truck, working on the engine.

Charlotte let out another low sigh as she opened the back door of her car and looked at the mess of pies. *So much work put to waste.* Guilt pressed like bricks on her shoulder blades. *And what a waste of food.*

As Charlotte picked up one of the strawberry pies, some of the filling got on her finger. She licked it off and figured maybe she'd even take time for a piece. It was good. Real good.

She called out to the guys. "Hey, do you two think you can give me a hand for a minute?"

Bob looked up, slightly irritated, but his face softened when he noticed the smashed pie in Charlotte's hands.

She held it up higher for him to get a good look. "I need help carrying these in."

"Can we have a piece when we're done?" Bob asked.

Hearing that, Pete glanced over too. "Is that strawberry?" He dropped his wrench in the top of the large red toolbox and wiped his hands on his jeans as he strode over. His eyes twinkled as he took it from Charlotte's hands.

"Yes, it's strawberry. And yes, you can have a piece when you're done helping me."

Hearing that, Bob wiped his brow with a blue handkerchief, and then sidled up to Charlotte and Pete. "What happened to it? It looks like someone's already taken a big fork to it."

"Yeah, what happened?" Pete rubbed his brow. "Weren't you using those pie carriers I made you?" Pete stuck his dirty finger into the pie and grabbed a big piece of crust. "Actually, maybe I'm glad you didn't use it."

Bob mumbled something under his breath and shook his head as he grabbed two pies.

"What a mess," he grumbled loud enough for them to hear.

"I know. I was taking my pies to Rosemary's and a lamb ran in front of my car. I slammed on the brakes—"

"And the pies went flying," Pete chuckled. "Sorry Mom. I know it's not funny, really it's not, especially since you know better than to transport them like that. But, boy, they're tasty. I think I'll have pie for lunch." He picked up another smashed piece and hurried to the house quickly, as if knowing his words were getting him into more trouble by the minute.

Bob started to the house, and Charlotte followed.

"Guess I know what I'll be doing tonight, replacing those pies—after we get home from this afternoon's fair board meeting, of course."

"Do you still have enough ingredients left?" Bob stomped up the porch steps, adding under his breath, "You've already been to the store twice this week, Charlotte."

"I think I do, actually, but I'll have to check."

Bob didn't answer, but Charlotte noticed his teeth clenching and his jaw tightening. More than one time over the past week he'd complained about how expensive everything was, and about their dwindling savings account.

Okay, Lord, here we go again. More unanticipated expenses, but I know you own the cattle on a thousand hills. I know you can provide.

"Grandma, may I have a piece?" Emily gingerly set the

camera bag on the dining room table and watched as they set the damaged pies on the counter.

"Sure, why not. I'm not anticipating time to make much of a lunch—or a big dinner tonight for that matter— so eat up." Charlotte waved a hand over the pies.

Emily's eyes widened as she scanned the varieties. "Mmm, this peach one looks good." She took a plate from the cupboard and cut herself a large, half-smashed piece.

"Mmm," she said, taking a bite. Her lips curled upward in pleasure. Seeing her response, Pete cut himself a piece of the same one, sliding it onto a chipped yellow plate.

"So, Em, are you going to bake something for the fair booth? Or maybe something to enter into the baking competition?" Pete elbowed her in the ribs.

"Are you kidding? I had enough baking last Thanksgiving."

"You mean you don't have *anything* to enter? Grandma let you get away with that?" Pete shook his head. "In my day, that wasn't allowed. For as long as I can remember, the weeks getting ready for the fair meant seeing how many entries I could come up with. In fact, one year, when I was seven, I remember staying up after midnight to work on a Lego project. I think I made a Noah's ark. That was my first entry ever."

"Yes, I think you're right. It was a large rectangle with Lego animals." Bob smiled.

"Yes, and remember how Pete was the only one who could figure out what they all were?" Charlotte leaned against the counter. "But it was a great first attempt and worthy of a blue ribbon in your age division. In fact, I still have your ribbon for that, and the one you got for the waxed-paper crayon drawing."

In her mind's eye Charlotte pictured the stocky little boy Pete used to be with light hair and large, round eyes. Eyes similar to Denise's and Emily's.

"Well, I was going to enter some new clothes I've been thinking of, but I didn't get them finished in time. When I was at Fabrics and Fun I completely forgot to get more fabric. Thread and buttons don't do any good without something to sew them on. Of course, maybe I can enter some photographs with the camera Aunt Rosemary gave me."

"She gave you a camera?" Bob glanced toward Charlotte for confirmation.

"Yes, Jerome's old camera. Your sister thinks Emily has an artistic eye, and she wants to encourage it."

"That was nice of her." Bob cut a piece of pie, nodding his head. "My sister always did enjoy doing something special for our kids and grandkids."

Emily finished her pie and then washed her hands, and pulled a roll of film out of the bag. "Wow, I don't even know how to load this. Mom had a digital camera, but she was afraid I'd break it. I've pretty much only taken photos with my phone."

"I can help." Pete patted his belly, signaling he'd had enough pie. "With my stomach filled up, I think my body has pretty much decided it's ready for a break from farm-work. I can show you how to load the film, and then we can head outside and snap some shots."

"Okay!" Emily said brightly.

Pete took the camera from the bag. Bob cut another thin piece of pie, and Charlotte waved a finger in his direction, which he promptly ignored.

Pete lifted the camera, looked through the viewfinder, and pretended to take a photo of Emily's face. Emily grinned, and then stuck out her tongue.

"You know, I like your idea of entering a photo at the fair. I can give you a few hints about the competition," he said.

Emily nodded. "Okay. What do they look for to get a blue ribbon?"

Pete opened the back of the camera and loaded the film. "They look for everything from interesting subject matter to focus and composition."

He set the camera on the table. "Oh, and they also look out for something called the law of thirds, which is just a fancy way of saying that things look more proportional when they're balanced into thirds."

"Huh? Okay, Uncle Pete, can you say that whole thing in English now?"

"Yeah, Pete, English please," Charlotte winked at him.

Pete's face scrunched and his eyes narrowed as if he were mimicking a professor giving a lecture. "That just means moving your center of focus off to one side, or up and down. For example, if you're taking a picture of a flower, don't set the flower right in the middle."

"Okay," Emily nodded. "But I still don't understand the thirds thing."

"Okay, how about this . . ." Pete glanced around the room. "Think of the picture you're taking as a window divided into panes." He pointed to the kitchen window. "See the two horizontal lines dividing the window into thirds, and the two vertical lines dividing it into thirds the other way? The focal point of the picture should be along one of those lines or where those lines intersect.

Centering an object doesn't usually make the most interesting photograph."

Emily stared out the kitchen window. She scooted from one side to another, as if adjusting the view of the barn through the window pane. "Yeah, okay, that makes sense now. I can see it. Cool!"

Bob eyed the camera. "Are you sure Emily should enter this year? With digital cameras people can take two hundred shots to get a good one. Two hundred shots on that thing will cost a lot of money for film and developing."

"Well, Aunt Rosemary already bought me some film, and I have some money saved up I could use for developing."

"It's worth a try." Charlotte commented. "Personally, I think Emily will do great. We've seen from her sewing that she has an eye for detail and composition. Besides, one thing Aunt Rosemary said is that she hated the thought of the camera not being used. I think she'll be excited to hear that Emily took some shots with the intention of entering some into the fair."

Pete handed the camera to Emily. She held it up to her face and looked through the viewfinder. "Ready, Uncle Pete?"

"Sure thing."

They headed out to the horse corral, and Charlotte watched from the window as Emily shot photos of the horses with Pete directing her. Charlotte knew she needed to check the pantry to see if she had enough flour and shortening to make six more pies. If she needed something she'd have to get it after the fair board meeting.

Charlotte considered calling Hannah to ask if she'd

come over and help—baking was always more fun when done with a friend—but then changed her mind. Hannah entered dozens of projects, and she was most likely putting her finishing touches on them even now.

Charlotte also considered calling Bill and taking him up on his offer to help on the fair board. Last year he'd stepped in and filled their shoes on the board, and he'd offered to do it again if the need ever came up. Charlotte wondered during times like these why they'd ever taken those "shoes" back.

Charlotte sighed, but she didn't budge. Her feet ached, her shoulders complained, and her head throbbed.

"I'll make a grocery list in a few minutes," she mumbled to herself. She made her way to the dining room table, and then folded her arms on the table and rested her forehead on her arms. She'd almost drifted off to sleep when the roar of Bob's truck engine revving outside stirred her.

"No rest for the weary." She rose and checked the pantry, thankful she had more flour, shortening, and apples than she thought, which meant she didn't have to worry about stopping by the grocery store on the way home. She hated the thought of going into town twice in one day, but today she had no choice.

Charlotte carried a basket of apples to the sink and rinsed them off, placing them on a dishtowel on the counter. Out the window she noticed Pete and Emily had moved to the garden to photograph the sunflowers. Emily's laughter carried on the wind as she focused the camera and snapped. Pete nodded and pointed, and Charlotte wished she could be out there with them, enjoying the late afternoon warmth and appreciating the scent of the late summer flowers on the breeze. But she had fifteen minutes to get cleaned up before they needed to head back to town for the meeting.

Tomorrow's another day. Tomorrow I'll have time to relax, rest, and enjoy the end of summer.

AS THEY DROVE BACK into town that afternoon, Emily fingered the roll of film in her hand as if it were a priceless gem. "Grandma, so what do I do when I print the photos? Do I put them in a photo album? And what does it mean to enter something in the fair?"

Charlotte glanced over at her granddaughter, trying to get her thoughts off Bob, who was home taking a "short nap" before joining her at the fair board meeting. She doubted his nap would be short. Her guess was that he was feeling sluggish after eating two pieces of pie.

She released the breath she'd been holding and loosened her grip on the steering wheel, attempting to forget her frustration over the fact that on top of not caring for himself properly, Bob continued to get on her case about the cost of food. Yet he felt perfectly okay driving his own truck to town for the board meeting and using up extra fuel when he could have ridden with her if he'd just been willing to go in a few minutes early so Emily could drop off the film. He claimed he needed to take the truck so he could check the engine after they'd been working on it, but Charlotte knew he just wanted a few more zzz's.

"Oh, to enter things into the fair . . . no, you don't use

albums. You'll have to enlarge those photos and frame them." Charlotte felt the hot, Nebraska sun beating down on her, and she turned up the air conditioning, wishing it worked better.

"So does the photo place do the enlargements? And I'm not sure what to do about frames . . ." Emily let her voice trail off, and Charlotte could see the eagerness that her granddaughter had felt earlier was already fading.

"Well, they have a machine that enlarges the photos. And as for a frame, I'm sure there are some in the attic you can use. But we don't have to worry about that now."

"So what does it mean when you enter something? Do I have to walk around with the framed pictures just like kids walk around with lambs?"

Charlotte's lip curled into a smile, and she chided herself for not giving Emily more information sooner. "No, it doesn't quite work like that. You see, there are many different ways items are entered, and different categories. Kids that are in 4-H compete with each other. And everyone else enters something called 'open class.' Starting Sunday, the fair starts accepting different entries."

"On Sunday? But I thought the fair didn't open until Tuesday."

"Well, the fair itself and the carnival rides open on Tuesday, but a lot of things happen before that to get the fair ready. I'm pretty sure Sunday is the day you'll have to submit your pictures—if you find one you like, that is."

"Sunday? I can't get things ready by Sunday. It's already Friday!" Emily dropped the canister of film on her lap as if also dropping her resolve to enter.

"Sure you can. There might be a photo you like in this first batch. Or you can take more photos tonight and we can get them developed tomorrow."

Emily nodded, but she still had a look of uncertainty in her gaze.

"Then, after you enter," Charlotte continued, hoping to recapture Emily's zeal, "your pictures will be displayed with the others in the arts and crafts building. Judges will give each winner a ribbon, and then when the gates open those buildings fill up as everyone comes in to check out the entries and winners."

"Yeah, well, Uncle Pete says that most of the time people visit those buildings to cool off from the hot sun outside."

Charlotte chuckled, "That's true for some, but I'd dare to say that most people go to support their friends and to see the displays. It's one of my favorite parts of the fair."

"Not mine. My favorite part is going to be Shae Lynne's concert."

"Oh, you know that already, do you—even more than the rides, the food, and hanging out with your friends?"

"Yes, totally. Are you kidding? She's one of my favorite singers. I think you'll really like her too."

"I keep telling myself I'm going to have to sit down and listen to her songs sometime. It seems everyone knows about her but me," Charlotte said.

"Remind me tomorrow, and I'll let you listen to my CD. I have it at home."

"Tomorrow? Why not tonight?" Charlotte slowed as she neared town, surprised for the second time today how busy the roads had become as everyone arrived early to prepare for the fair.

Emily sighed. "Because I'm staying at Ashley's again tonight, remember?"

"Oh, yes, I remember now. I sort of forgot about that after the lamb-and-pie fiasco. Are you sure you want to stay again? I mean, you can stay home tonight and help your dear ol' grandma make some pies." Charlotte winked at Emily.

Emily bit her lip, and Charlotte could tell she was conflicted. "Actually, I wanted to stay with Ashley because she says things get crazy when the fair starts. She has to help her mom at work, and she's lucky to get even one night off to go to the fair. But maybe I can help you bake tomorrow."

"No problem. Don't worry. Enjoy your time with your friend. And, yes, I'll remind you when you get home about that CD. I just have to find out what all the fuss is about."

Chapter Three

S weet," Sam muttered as he busted out a backside 360 ollie, flying off the curb and landing in the parking lot, rolling to a stop.

"Dude, do it again." Paul crossed his arms over his husky chest.

"Seriously? Did you miss it the first time?" Sam called over his shoulder, tossing his head to get his bangs out of his eyes. "Maybe you should get some glasses." Yet even as Sam said the words he picked up his skateboard and carried it to the sidewalk to try again.

He'd spent the night at Paul's house and promised his Uncle Pete he'd meet him at the feed store by three o'clock. Uncle Pete claimed he needed help loading stuff in the truck, but Sam knew the truth. Pete just wanted to make sure he was around to do the evening chores.

Finding the right spot to launch, Sam kicked off on his board. He set his front foot right behind the front trucks and the ball of his back foot on the toe edge of his board, at the base of his board's tail. As he rolled near the edge of the curb, he bent his knees and wound up his shoulders.

Just before the front wheels hit the curb, Sam turned his shoulders and arms the opposite way from his spin, winding up tight, feeling as if he were ready to explode.

Sam reached the curb and ollied hard, very hard.

Adrenaline pumped through him. His heart pounded, and his body felt hot with excitement as he hung in the air. He scooped his skateboard with his back foot, spinning the board in the same direction he was moving. A second later, Sam bent his knees, preparing for the landing. As smooth as butter, his feet reconnected with the board and the board with the ground. Cheers rose from Paul. Jake cheered too, waving his long, lanky arms in the air. Sam also heard female voices cheering. Heat rushed to his cheeks.

Sam turned and spotted Emily and Arielle sitting under a tall oak on the lawn. They clapped and cheered, and Sam waved a hand their direction as if to say it was no big deal. Yet inwardly he was pleased Arielle had seen him nailing his best 360 yet.

He kicked off again, riding down the sidewalk, zipping closer to where Emily and Arielle sat on the grass.

"What are you doing here?" he called.

"Grandma is over at the fairgrounds for a meeting," Emily said. "I dropped off a roll of film to get developed at the one-hour photo place. Ashley has to work for another hour, and I saw Arielle in town waiting for her dad. We were just walking around wasting time; then we saw you guys and headed over."

Sam crossed his arms over his chest. "Cool. I—"

"Oh look, horses!" Arielle interrupted. She jumped to

her feet and hurried across the parking lot to where two guys were unloading horses from a horse trailer.

Sam watched as his sister followed his girlfriend, a camera in her hands.

Sam glanced over to Paul and Jake, who didn't seem as excited that the girls had shown up. They continued skating, trying to land a 360 ollie themselves. They motioned for Sam to join them, but instead he kicked up his skateboard, caught it, and walked after the girls. Arielle and Emily stood to the side as they watched the men with the horses. Sam stood behind them. The cowboys took a dark brown quarter horse with a white nose out of the trailer first. Next came a gray Appaloosa.

"Wow, what beautiful horses." Arielle tucked her hands into the pockets of her jean shorts. "What are their names?"

"Rimrock and Stetson," answered a tall, thin cowboy wearing a black hat.

"Which one's which?" Arielle inched forward, and Sam tried not to act jealous. He didn't like the fact she was ignoring him and talking to these guys.

"The dark brown one is Rimrock. The speckled one is Stetson."

"They are so beautiful," Arielle called.

"They look strong," Emily added.

"So where are you from?" Sam called.

"Omaha." The cowboy with the black hat turned to his friend. "How long did it take us to get here, two hours? Three?"

"At least." The shorter cowboy walked over with the speckled horse on a lead, stretching out its legs. "And then they told us that we can't get into the fairgrounds today," he complained.

"Do you mind if I take their pictures?" Emily asked.

"I don't mind if you promise you'll come to the barrel races and cheer for us." He tilted his hat back on his head, dabbing his forehead with his handkerchief.

"Oh, please. If you'll cheer for us," Sam mimicked under his breath.

Arielle turned as if just remembering he was there. She sidled up to him and placed her hand on his back. "Have you ever seen barrel races?"

"No. Can't say I have."

She chuckled. "Well, we need to get some country into you, city boy."

He reached behind and took her hand, holding it in his. Her hand was small and soft, and holding it made him smile.

Emily snapped a photo of the cowboy leading the horse. She walked close to him, looking up at him. "My friend Hunter is gonna ride in those races. He's good. I've seen him practice."

Emily turned to Sam. "We can all go together. It will be fun."

"Nah, I don't think I'm gonna be at the fair much."

Arielle's eyebrows shot up as she glanced up at him. "Why not?"

"The fair? Are you serious?" he scoffed.

"What's wrong with the fair?" Arielle's voice rose an octave. "You're not saying you're too good for the fair, are you?" She pulled her hand away from his.

Sam dropped the skateboard and pushed it back and forth with his foot. He raised his hands. "Hey, no offense. It's just that—"

"It's just that his friend Jordan is gonna be here," Emily butted in. "He's from San Diego, and Sam's afraid he's gonna think the fair is lame. Afraid that Jordan will go back to San Diego and tell everyone how stupid Nebraska is."

Sam crossed his arms over his chest. "Yeah, we're just going to skateboard and stuff instead."

"Sam Slater, that's the dumbest thing I've ever heard. You'd rather hang around a parking lot and jump in the air instead of spending the week having fun and hanging out with your friends? I bet Jake and Paul are going." Arielle called to them and motioned them over. "Jake, Paul!"

They skated over and looked at her expectantly.

"Yeah?" Paul asked.

"Are you guys going to the fair?"

"Of course," Paul shrugged. "Why?"

Arielle placed a hand on Sam's arm. "Because Sam doesn't want to go, and I'm trying to talk him into it."

"Oh, I never said I didn't want to go. I just think Jordan won't want to."

"No, seriously, it's cool. Have you ever heard of the demolition derby?" Jake's eyes brightened.

"Yeah, man, they take these old cars, and they drive around and smash each other. Pieces of metal fly everywhere," Paul added.

"Well, I guess that doesn't sound so bad." Sam shrugged, not letting on that it actually sounded cool.

"And don't forget the rodeo," one of the cowboys said,

hoisting a bucket of feed from the back of the horse trailer. The muscles in his arms bulged as he carried it and then poured it into a pile on the asphalt parking lot. "The rodeo isn't for wimps."

"Didn't say it was, sir." Sam lifted his hands, realizing he wasn't going to get out of this conversation easily.

Gee, thanks, Arielle. He glanced at her from the corner of his eye. As if reading his mind, she just grinned and shrugged.

"And remember the pig wrestling?" Jake said. "We were on a team last year and—"

"You mean you actually wrestle a pig?" Emily interrupted.

"Yeah, a big one." Paul spread his arms. "There is this pen with mud in it, and you have to run in there, pick up the pig, and drop it into a barrel in the middle."

"By yourself?" Emily asked. "That would be something fun to take pictures of!"

"No, you're on a team of four people. Sometimes the pigs pee in the mud and—"

"Dude, that seriously is the stupidest thing I've ever heard." Sam tried to hide his shocked smile behind his hand.

"Not if you win. It's a big deal. Last time the winners won a thousand bucks."

Sam scratched his head. "Wow. Just for picking up a pig and putting it in a barrel?"

"Yup." Arielle took his hand again. "Now you're interested, aren't you? See? I knew there would be a way to get you there. Now I know it's the pigs."

Sam shrugged. "I don't know. Maybe. It all depends on what Jordan wants to do."

"Maybe Jordan will want to join a pig-wrestling team. Maybe the four of us guys should do it together." Jake flipped his ball cap backward on his head.

"Well, for a thousand bucks . . ." Sam let his voice trail off as he imagined the ways he could spend that money. "Yeah, maybe."

Chapter
Four

Charlotte walked by Bob's side as they strolled under a large sign at the gate that read, WELCOME TO THE FAIR. She'd dropped Emily off at Kepler's Pharmacy and then arrived at the fairgrounds just as Bob was parking. His face looked red and flushed as he walked beside her, and she hoped it was only from the heat.

She readjusted her sun visor over her short, cropped hair and smiled as she took in the neatly trimmed grass of the Adams County fairground. The tension of the day almost seemed to melt from her shoulders as the excitement of another fair took its place. Workers moved around the grounds like ants on an anthill, delivering food items to the concession stands, cleaning out exhibition halls, pitching fresh hay into the barns.

In her mind's eye she imagined what it would be like in a few days when the people arrived. It would be a mix of cowpokes with pointy-toed boots and senior citizens in motorized wheelchairs. Little girls wearing pigtails and little boys in cowboy hats. Older boys strutting around trying to impress the girls, and girls doing the same, attempting to get the attention of the boys—as if they didn't already have it.

31

Walking in the warm sunshine, she slipped her hand into her husband's and again attempted to simply enjoy this brief moment of celebration between summer and fall. A time of fun before the work of harvest began. A time when everyone's attention was focused on who had the fattest pumpkin, the prettiest ear of corn, and the rosiest strawberries. One's hard work was weighed against his or her neighbor's efforts, but in a fun-loving way.

It was a time when big-city folks came down from Harding, and even some from Omaha, to focus on family and play. And Charlotte had to admit, fair evenings were her favorite time of the year to stroll and catch up with neighbors.

She and Bob slowed as they neared the fair office and waved to Arnold Humphrey, a member of their church, who was raking grass clippings into a large black garbage bag.

"Can you feel the excitement in the air?" Arnold paused and leaned on his rake.

"Hard to miss, Arnold." Bob waved.

Charlotte grinned. "Keep up the good work."

They slowed, and Bob opened the door. They entered, and Charlotte noticed the other board members already gathered around the table. She just hoped the agenda was short today. Although she'd already prepped the crusts for her pies, she had a lot of baking yet to do.

"With the extra money from the concert, I think we should modernize the fairgrounds," Dwayne Cook, a farmer who lived just a few miles from Heather Creek, was saying. "The RV area could use some new showers and maybe even an RV dumping station. It would be nice for folks if they could just take care of that here."

"And how about a new stage?" Hannah smoothed her hands across the table as if she were picturing it in her mind's eye. She paused to wave to Charlotte. "I heard that in Omaha they can put on quite a production."

"I don't know. I'm not sure if people would like that too much." Ned Patton, who had been on the fair board longer than Hannah had been alive, patted Hannah's hand to show he meant no offense. "It seems that people like coming and getting a glimpse of the American past. They like things the way they are. Why change them?"

"Yeah, I've heard people say that 'bit of American past' line before, and in my opinion it's just laziness. Should we let the fairgrounds crumble around us like all the soddies and old barns crumbling around the county?" Hannah jutted out her chin as Charlotte sat down beside her, feeling as if she should applaud her friend's vigor.

"Now, the fair isn't all about the big show," Ned's wife Betty said, her eyes appearing twice their size from behind her thick glasses. "It's about people getting together, rewarding one another for small accomplishments, gently competing. Right, Charlotte?"

Charlotte swallowed hard as all eyes turned in her direction. "Actually, I see points on both sides of the argument, and personally I think we need to strike a balance. There's a place for the quilts and the sunflower displays as much as there's a place for the demolition derby. Besides, is this really something we need to discuss *now*? Like I tell the kids, I don't think we should count our chickens before they hatch. Yes, I think it will be a great turnout, especially at the concert, but I vote to table this conversation for two weeks, until after all the grounds have been cleared, the bills have been paid, and our funds are totaled."

The room grew quiet. Out the window they had a view of the carnival workers setting up their rides on a large patch of dirt that would soon be transformed into a mechanical playground.

Finally, Dwayne Cook spoke up. "Yes, I understand, but I don't see how we won't make extra money. Shae Lynne is a popular young lady. As soon as the posters started going up we began getting calls in the office. Ticket sales are up. Some people are coming in all the way from Colorado."

"Oh my, I just love her song, 'You'll Miss Me When I'm Gone,'" Hannah said, humming a tune that sounded slightly familiar.

"Oh yes, but that's not my favorite," Betty piped up. "My favorite is 'Believe in Second Chances.'"

Charlotte looked at Betty in surprise. She had to be at least eighty, yet the elderly woman was more familiar with the rising country star than Charlotte was.

"What?" Betty asked. "I love listening to the radio when I'm canning."

"I must be the only one who's never heard of this woman." Charlotte shrugged.

"Sure you have." Betty cleared her throat. "Believe in second chances . . . because second chances believe in you," she sang with a quiver in her voice.

Charlotte smiled and nodded; she didn't have the heart to tell Betty she still didn't know the song. She didn't want to burst her bubble. Then, when everyone else around the table joined in, Charlotte wished she had a camcorder. There had never been a fair board meeting quite like this.

SAM WAS SKATING AROUND the parking lot of the feed store when he saw the familiar truck coming down the road. He waved to his uncle and skated over to the truck as Pete parked it. Pete's order was waiting for them, and it took less than ten minutes to load it up.

Pete patted Sam's shoulder. "Thanks for your strong back. I need to go pay my bill and then we'll be heading out in one minute."

Sam followed Pete into the store and checked out the baby ducks while Uncle Pete chatted with one of his friends. *So much for being done in one minute*. He brushed a finger over their yellow fluff and then he heard a snicker behind him.

Pete and his friend were eyeing a "cowboy" who had walked through the door. He looked the part, but it was clear from his outfit that his cowboy boots were right off the shelf. His Levi's still had the creases from where they'd been folded. His vest was bright, colorful. Too colorful. It looked like something one would see onstage, but not around Bedford. Sam couldn't help but chuckle too.

He watched as the man made his way up to the counter, but he couldn't hear the conversation over the squawking of the baby ducks. Sam rose and walked closer, pretending he was checking out the rack of postcards near the front counter. Country music played on the staticky radio, and Sam couldn't help but shudder. He didn't understand how people actually listened to that stuff.

"Yeah, I know a perfect spot," the man behind the counter was saying. "Heather Creek Farm is a pretty place. In fact it just won an award. Was named Adams County Farm of the Year, or somethin' like that. In fact..." The clerk pointed. "The owner of the farm is right over there."

The man turned and approached Pete. Sam sauntered over, eager to know what this was about.

"Are you Pete? I'm William Taylor, up from Nashville. So, I hear that you have an amazing farm." The man thrust his hand in Pete's direction.

"Well, I think so, but what's this about?" Pete shook the man's hand reluctantly.

"Oh, sorry. How rude of me. Let me explain. I'm here to shoot a video—a music video, to be exact, and it sounds like your farm is just the type of place I'm looking for."

At the mention of a music video, Sam's eyes widened. He elbowed his uncle. "You're going to do it, aren't you?"

Pete removed his cap and scratched his head. "I don't think that's a good idea. I'm pretty sure Dad won't appreciate a bunch of people roaming around the place. Heck, he follows me around and keeps an eye on everything *I* do. I can't imagine him letting strangers on the farm, doing who knows what, and shooting a video to boot."

"Uncle Pete." Sam grabbed his uncle's arm. "Shouldn't you think about this?"

"Heck, I'll let you use *my* farm." A man's voice called from the next aisle over.

Pete laughed. "Yeah, see?" He pointed to the other

farmer. "There you go. Problem solved." Then Pete turned to Sam. "Ready, Sam?"

"Are you sure?"

But Pete strode out the door, and Sam had no choice but to follow. The ride home was silent, as if Uncle Pete was deep in thought.

Finally, Sam couldn't keep it in. "I don't understand. What are you thinking? Our farm could be famous."

"Sam, were you just born yesterday? Did you see that guy? He was some type of scam artist. Someone from Nashville wouldn't be dressed like that. He probably came in with the carnival and is trying to pull a fast one on someone. Who knows what would happen if you let a guy like that on your property? Why, I saw on one of those investigation shows that people come on your property, pretend to be hurt, and then sue you for the whole thing."

"But what if it's true, Uncle Pete? What if he *is* here to do a music video? What if . . ." Sam's eyes widened. "What if the video is for Two Dead Brothers? They're a rocking group."

Pete glanced over at Sam and cocked an eyebrow. "You really think that rock-and-roll group you like would be filming in Bedford, Nebraska? In fact, what music star comes here?" Pete paused and scratched his head. "Actually, that one country singer's coming to town. What if it's for her?"

"Shae Lynne? Ugh, not country music."

"Your sister likes that Shae Lynne chick. Dana too." Pete looked in his rearview mirror as if he was considering turning the car around. Then he shook his head. "Oh well, it's probably too late now."

Sam leaned against the door and put his elbow out the window, letting the breeze hit his face, cooling him off. "I'm sure it was Shae Lynne. Good thing you didn't say yes. Jordan feels the same about country music as I do. I mean, who really likes to listen to songs about dead dogs, pickup trucks, and dudes whining about the girl who got away?"

"Yeah, you're right." Pete chuckled. "Let some other poor sap deal with that."

～ Chapter
Five

C harlotte took a sip of her iced tea and glanced over
the list of fair activities in the newspaper, chuckling
to herself about how much folks around Bedford
liked to "pull."

Bush Pullers Tractor Pull
4-H Shows & Exhibits
Live Entertainment
Antique Tractor Pull
Mutton Busting
Parade
Commercial Exhibits
Pedal Pull
Chainsaw Artist
Coloring Contest
Semitruck Pull
Midway Carnival

She tossed the newspaper aside and set to work peeling
and coring apples. As she worked, the song "Believe in
Second Chances" replayed in her mind. The tune had stuck

after some of the fair board members sang it. Then, to her surprise, it had come on the radio during her drive home.

It was a nice song, she supposed. The tune was catchy, at least. Charlotte made a mental note to ask Sam later about the words. Even if he didn't listen to that music, surely he'd be able to find the lyrics on the computer. She would've asked Emily, but she was spending the night at Ashley's house. And Christopher, Charlotte knew, followed country music about as closely as his grandmother did.

Charlotte continued to hum as she worked, and later her steps felt a bit lighter as she walked to the pantry for a few jars of cherries. *Three apple pies and three cherry-berries. That should be enough.*

As she gathered up all the ingredients, she also thought through her to-do list—getting out bedding for Jordan's visit, rechecking the times she was supposed to work at the church's pie booth, and marking off items she'd be entering into the fair: jars of apple pie filling, pickles, beets, that embroidery project, a wildflower bouquet, some of the sunflowers . . .

Most days Charlotte enjoyed baking, but today she wasn't in the mood. She just hoped that by the time she started rolling out the pie crusts she'd prepped earlier, the desire would hit her.

"Ma Mildred," she mumbled to herself, picturing her mother-in-law's face, "if I'd known what we were starting that first day you taught me to roll out a pie crust, I might have declined." She smiled at the memory of that day long ago, appreciating it even though no one else was around.

"Talking to yourself again?" Bob's voice called from the living room, and Charlotte saw her husband yawn and stretch as he made his way into the kitchen. It was clear from his rumpled hair and glassy eyes that he'd fallen asleep after getting home from the fair board meeting. Sometimes she wished she had thirty minutes to lie down for a quick nap too.

"Yes, I'm talking to myself again, and I'm a good companion. I always answer what I want to hear, and I never disagree." Charlotte smiled.

Bob scratched his cheek and sniffed the air. "What's for dinner again?"

"I'm just making sandwiches since I have to get these pies done." She took a sip from her tea on the counter.

"No dinner?" From Bob's furrowed brow Charlotte could tell he wasn't pleased with the idea of not getting a hearty meal of meat and potatoes.

"I'll make sandwiches. They'll have to be good enough for tonight. I have to replace those pies I ruined, remember?"

"I thought you weren't going to do that."

"No, I told you I was."

"Well, then make an extra pie for me," Bob wrapped an arm around her shoulder.

"I think you've had enough pie today. Remember those two big pieces you had before you lay down? They were loaded with sugar. Speaking of which, we need to remember to set a date for your checkup with Dr. Carr."

Bob waved a hand in the air. "I'm fine. I'm watching myself. Besides, the two pieces of pie I had were small," he snapped, and Charlotte realized she was doing it again, treating Bob like a child. He *had* been doing better at checking his sugar and watching what he ate.

He's my husband, not one of my grandkids, she chided

herself. She set the apple she was peeling in the colander and then rinsed off her hands. She turned and wrapped her arms around Bob. He smelled like outdoors mixed with diesel, and she was thankful for that. Thankful to have him around. Thankful she didn't have to talk to herself all day.

Bob gave her a quick hug in return, and then pulled back and walked over to the window to look outside.

"I still don't think you should worry about replacing those pies," he mumbled. "Why don't we just put some money into the till? You've been working too hard lately, with all you do for the kids, the church booth, the fair board."

"That does seem easier, but you know they're counting on the pies. Plus, I'd like to keep our cash for the fair itself," she said. "We'll be having our three grandkids plus Jordan running around there, wanting to eat that expensive fair food and go on rides. I'll be fine. I won't worry about trying to match the original pies. I'm just making some apple-caramel and cherry-berries and calling that good. I didn't have to buy anything. I'm just using what we have on hand."

Bob didn't argue, although Charlotte could sense he was a little stressed. She didn't even want to mention the back-to-school shopping they needed to do as soon as the fair was over.

Charlotte began humming that country tune again, hoping to brighten Bob's mood. He poured himself a large glass of milk and then sat down to watch Charlotte work.

Bob finished the milk in two gulps and then got back up and set the glass on the counter. "I chatted with Henry

Dodd from the gas station yesterday, and he's pretty excited about that country singer coming in. Hopes it will boost sales. He heard she was over at a fair in Iowa and the tickets nearly sold out. There were also 20 percent more attendees than the previous year."

"Yeah, Emily and Ashley seem pretty excited. They said that even kids who don't usually listen to country music like her, although I'm so far out of the loop I have a hard time remembering her name." Charlotte sliced the apples she had cored.

"Doesn't matter if we remember. What counts is that I have a feeling this is going to be our best fair yet."

"The fair with flair," Charlotte said, repeating the slogan they'd chosen. She hummed more of Shae Lynne's song as she finished slicing the apples. The smallest hint of a smile touched her lips.

WITH THREE PIES IN THE OVEN, Charlotte decided to stretch her legs and get some fresh air. Toby trotted by her side as she eyed the sunflowers, trying to decide which ones she should cut and enter in the floral competition. Not that she'd cut them yet. There were still a couple of days before the floral displays needed to be in, which was a good thing.

Christopher had run out to join Pete and Sam, helping them unload from their trip to the feed store. Bob was in the barn finishing up afternoon chores. A bird sang from the branches of the nearest tree, and the sunflowers swayed in the breeze as if following along.

Charlotte gently touched the stiff fuzz on the stalk of one of the sunflowers. Most of the huge blooms stood taller than she did, and she had a hard time picking out the best blossoms since the flowers' heads were lifted toward the sun. Maybe she could get Bob to help her look at them later.

The sound of car tires on the gravel interrupted her thoughts. Charlotte turned and watched as a black sedan with a rental car sticker on the door pulled into the driveway and parked. A thin man with dark Levi's and a colorful cowboy vest climbed from the car. As Charlotte stepped out of the garden area and walked toward the car, the man waved.

Hearing the sound of the car, Bob exited the barn. With a wide smile, the man strode over to him. Charlotte was sure she'd never seen him before. In fact, he didn't look like he was from Nebraska. He had the quick walk of a city fellow on a mission.

Charlotte folded her arms over her chest and joined Bob.

"Hello there. I would guess you are Mr. and Mrs. Stevenson? The nice fellow from the feed store sent me over." He stretched out his hand and Bob shook it. Then he turned to Charlotte.

She shook his hand too. It was soft and small, not like Bob's large work hands.

"Yes, we're the Stevensons. How can we help?" she asked.

The man whistled. "Sure is a pretty place you have here. Heard it won Nebraska's farm of the year."

Charlotte glanced at Bob, and she could tell from his scowl that he didn't like the man's indirect approach.

"Adams County farm of the year actually, Mr.—I'm sorry, we didn't get your name." Bob tilted his head.

"Taylor, William Taylor with BNC Media, but you can call me Will."

"Sure, Will. I'm Bob and this is Charlotte. Did you say you're with the media?"

"A media group. We design sets for shoots, work with talent scouts, and we're actually here in Bedford to shoot a video."

"Oh, like a documentary?" Charlotte tapped Bob's arm. "Remember that one we watched on farming—"

Will laughed. "Oh no. Not on farming. We're here to shoot a music video. You know, the kind they show on CMT—Country Music Television."

"I can't say I've heard of that before." Bob lifted his hands, as if putting a barrier between him and the man. "But I can say that there won't be any rock concerts happening on my farm."

"Oh no." Will laughed again, and Charlotte noted humor in his gaze. "It's for a country music video. And this is just the type of *country* I'm looking for."

"Really? We appreciate that, but—" Charlotte started.

Will continued talking, cutting her off. "Yes, there's some beautiful country in these parts, which made us think this area is where we need to film it."

Bob stroked his chin. "Yes, well, I'm not sure we can help you."

"Sure you can. You see, part of my job is to scout a location. By this I mean look for the most dramatic, picturesque place we can find. And it needs to fit the story we're trying to create, of course. I just got in today, and I need to find a place as soon as possible." Will grinned again.

Charlotte's mind worked to keep up with what he was saying. "And just how can we help you?"

"Well, we were looking for someplace special near Bedford. Someplace not too far from town. Someplace we can get our trucks in and out of. And someplace that will shout, 'Home Sweet Home.'" Will spread his arms wide. "And, folks, I think I've found it."

"Heather Creek?" Bob looped his thumbs through the suspenders on his overalls. "I don't think that will work. You see, this is a real farm. Those are real crops out there in the fields. We have real animals to care for."

"Exactly! That's why I'm so interested. We don't want a backstage set for this video. We want our viewers to feel like they've come home to the place their heart—"

"I think what my husband is trying to say," Charlotte interrupted, "is that we have to make sure the farm runs well. We live off this land. We can't have people running around here, trampling our crops or getting in the way of our chores. If anything goes wrong, it means we don't eat this winter."

"Of course. I completely understand. My own grandfather was raised on a farm in Kansas. I've heard the stories. I know what it's like."

Bob eyed the man, and Charlotte could tell that her husband wasn't impressed by him—or by the idea he was describing.

She offered Will a friendly smile but spoke in a firm tone. "Yes, well, there are plenty of other farms around Bedford. Some are really nice. I'm sure you'll find one you like."

"My wife is right," Bob said. "I'm sure there are others who would be happy to be involved. It's just that this is a busy farm and an especially busy week. We don't need any more excitement right now."

Will wildly nodded and then rubbed his hands together. "Of course, I know you probably have a lot of questions. Maybe we should sit and I can explain the process . . ."

Charlotte felt tension building in the back of her neck. "I'm sorry, but I believe my husband has already given you our answer. It just won't work. The answer is no."

"Are you sure?" Will offered the same frown Christopher gave her when he wasn't allowed a second piece of dessert. "I mean, this is quite an opportunity. There's a nice payment for—"

Charlotte let out a heavy sigh. "I don't know how we can make it clearer that we're not interested."

"Besides, how do we know this is for real?" Bob asked, continuing her response. "That *you're* for real? I mean, we've never heard of this type of thing before."

Will chuckled to himself. "I guarantee that when big trucks and trailers with equipment, people, and props show up, you'll know for sure that this is the real thing. And of course when Shae Lynne shows up—"

"Shae Lynne? The video is for her?" Charlotte wondered if she'd heard right.

"Yes, Shae Lynne. I wasn't going to tell you until we knew for sure you'd accept. She draws large crowds. And if the word gets out, well, you can imagine."

Charlotte pictured her grandchildren's responses if they were to tell them Shae Lynne would be visiting their farm. "Bob, can you imagine what Emily would say?"

Will didn't comment. He just smiled.

Bob looked at Charlotte, and Charlotte looked at Bob. She could see the gears turning in his mind, and she wondered what he was thinking.

"Can you wait until morning for an answer?" Bob rubbed his chin, leaving a smudge of dirt on his jaw line. "I'd like to pray about it."

Will's broad smile faded, and he tilted his head and looked at Bob as if that were the last thing he'd expected to hear. "Pray about it. Yes sir. Yes, that would be fine." Will glanced at his watch. "I just want you to know that I'll have to look around at other farms. I can't waste any time, in case you say no for sure. I mean, if another farm says yes I'll have to go with them."

Charlotte crossed her arms over her chest. "Yes, we understand, and if you find someplace else, then we'll take that as an answer that it wasn't God's will for us after all."

Will tucked his thumbs into his vest pockets and glanced around again, as if suddenly unsure what to do or say. "It sure is a beautiful farm," he said again.

Charlotte placed her hand in Bob's. "Yes, we think it is. The Lord has provided greatly."

"Okay, then." Will removed his cowboy hat and wiped his sleeve across his brow. "If you don't mind, then, I can call you in the morning."

"Sure, that will be fine." Charlotte gave him their number, and he wrote it on his palm with a pen.

Then Will handed his card to Charlotte. "My cell phone number's on there. Feel free to call if you come to a decision sooner."

"We will." Bob reached out and shook Will's hand again.

"Thank you." Will ambled back to his car, and then with one last wave he drove away.

Charlotte and Bob waved back, and then Charlotte glanced up at her husband.

"I don't think he expected your answer. I'm sure it's not what he hears every day. So what do you think, Bob?"

"Well, Char, I know what I think. It's an odd request, and we have enough going on this week as it is, but as I told the man, I need to pray about it and see what God thinks. It's an unusual-enough request to make me wonder. I mean, out of all the farms in Nebraska . . ."

"You're right. We should ask the Lord."

Bob turned his gaze toward Heather Creek. "I think I'm going to take a walk down to the creek. Would you like to join me?"

Charlotte glanced at her watch. "Oh no! My pies! They were supposed to be out of the oven five minutes ago!" She hurried to the house. "I'm sorry, Bob. I wish I could join you."

Bob said something, but his words were lost in the slamming of the screen door. The warm scent of apples, cherries and browning pie crust hit Charlotte's face as she entered the kitchen.

Oh please, oh please let them not be burned.

BOB TAPPED HIS TOOTHBRUSH on the side of the sink three times and then slid it into the holder.

"I don't know, Char. I've wanted to call that Nashville

fellow a dozen times to tell him no thanks, but something keeps holding me back."

"Some*thing* or some*one*?" Charlotte patted her freshly washed face with a towel.

"Good question." Bob shrugged. "Although what Pete said makes sense."

"About the guy being sneaky and coming to you after Pete had already said no?"

"Yeah. Then again, Pete didn't have a right to say no. It's not his farm. It's ours. And the fact is, the spring rains pushed back planting and the crops aren't as good as they could be. And that fellow mentioned that there would be payment involved. A little extra money would be nice."

He strode out of the bathroom and Charlotte followed, flipping off the light.

"I know. It does sound like an unexpected gift, but I'm worried about the influence on the kids," she said. "All those music and video people hanging around. I mean, what do we know about them? Who knows what kind of lifestyles they lead? The kids are finally settling down on the farm. Will this disrupt everything?"

Bob looked out the bedroom window at the night sky filled with stars, gazing with expectation as if hoping he'd find an answer there.

"Then again," Charlotte thought of her earlier conversation with Emily. "I'm not sure Emily would ever forgive us if we had the opportunity to have *the* Shae Lynne on our farm and we passed it up."

Bob slid under the sheets and folded his hands behind his head. "True, but we've never based our parenting on popularity."

Charlotte slid into bed beside him and flipped off the lamp on the nightstand. The window was open, and warm air, scented with roses, filtered into the room. The sounds of crickets and frogs from the creek drifted in too. She listened for a while, replaying all the options in her mind. Then she turned on her side and could tell from Bob's breathing that he hadn't fallen asleep yet.

"It's interesting to think that we live the type of life country singers try to portray on videos. Living off the land. Quiet nights listening to the crickets and summer afternoons sipping lemonade on the porch."

"Or eating homemade pie." Bob sighed.

Above them, Charlotte could hear Sam's footsteps in his bedroom. She guessed he was having a hard time sleeping, planning for his friend's arrival tomorrow.

Bob cleared his throat, interrupting Charlotte's thoughts. "You don't know this, but I've been praying for funds, for some type of help to keep up on the bills and to maybe put a little aside. You know, this is Sam's last year of high school, and we have very little college money saved up. And even though it's not what I would pick, it does seem like God is plopping something on us, dropping it out of the clear blue."

"You're right, Bob. We don't know how much money they have in mind, but every little bit helps." She stared at the ceiling, almost afraid to ask the next question. "So are you saying that you're going to tell the man yes? That we're going to do it?"

"I think so. It just doesn't seem like an opportunity like this comes from nowhere."

Charlotte patted her husband's arm and snuggled down,

but her mind was far from at ease with the idea. She closed her eyes and tried to take deep, cleansing breaths, as if willing herself to be all right with the thought of their farm being overrun by big-city folks.

Okay, Lord, I know this offer hasn't caught you by surprise. She smiled. *You have a way of stirring things up, don't you? Just give me peace, and please protect the hearts of these kids. And help my attitude, Lord. I can't imagine adding one more thing, especially this. Yet, show me what it means to love those different from me. Show me how to* . . . Charlotte yawned . . . *how to show off* you.

And with that last prayer deep in her mind, Charlotte drifted off.

Chapter Six

The scent of fresh rain filled the morning air, and Charlotte took her mug of coffee to the porch. Sitting on the top step, she shivered at the slight dampness from last night's shower, and with a contented sigh took in the sight of the freshly washed earth.

Today's a new day and your mercy is new every morning, Lord. Help me remember that.

The colors of summer—the green of the front lawn, the golds, reds, and purples of the flowers, the golden-green of the corn stalks—were more vibrant after the rain. Even the small puddles in the driveway glimmered with morning light as if not wanting to be outdone by the pink clouds above or the water droplets on the daisies near the front steps.

The sound of footsteps on the gravel and the barking dog told her the dynamic duo was approaching.

"Grandma, watch this." Christopher called. He was slightly short of breath, and his cheeks were flushed from running.

"Watch what?"

"Our training—you know, for showing Toby at the fair."

Charlotte patted Toby's soft brown ear and then leaned back, straightening her shoulders to show she was paying attention. "Okay, I'm watching."

Christopher pointed to Toby. "Sit."

A few feet from Charlotte, Toby sat.

Christopher backed up, taking slow, smooth steps across the damp front lawn, as if any quick movements might cause Toby to bolt. "Stay."

Toby cocked her head, watching Christopher, but to Charlotte's surprise, the dog stayed.

Finally, when Christopher reached the end of the lawn near the driveway, he motioned to Toby. Charlotte smiled as Toby trotted to Christopher. The dog approached with her tail wagging and jumped up, her front paws on Christopher's chest.

"Great job, Christopher! I'm impressed." Charlotte took another sip from her coffee.

"No, Toby. Sit!" Christopher took a step back, and Toby dropped again to all fours. "She's supposed to sit when she comes, not jump up on me. That's what I'm working on today."

"Well, from what I can see, you're on the right track." Charlotte set the coffee mug to the side, next to the railing, and stood. "Toby always follows me. She doesn't sit and stay like that at all."

Christopher nodded and smiled. "Yeah, she's getting the hang of it."

Charlotte walked toward Christopher. "You're doing great, but if I remember correctly you're supposed to turn your back on Toby when you walk across the ring. In fact,

I think there's also a rule about how far Toby's supposed to sit from your feet too. You might want to check in the training manual for the specific things you'll be tested on."

Christopher bit his lip and raised his eyebrows.

"You do have your manual, don't you?" Charlotte asked.

"Yeah, I have it . . ." Christopher's voice trailed off.

"And?"

Christopher reached down and ruffled Toby's fur. "And I sort of left it outside. It got rained on. The pages are all stuck together."

"So, what are you going to do about that?" Charlotte crossed her arms over her chest.

Christopher shrugged. "Just try to remember what the book said?"

"Or maybe you can ask someone for help? That's what family's all about, you know. It's not just about hiding our problems or trying to take care of everything ourselves."

"Grandma?" Christopher strode toward her. He wrapped his arms around her waist. "Next time you go in to the fair board, do you think you can pick up another manual for me?"

"Sure, Christopher. I'm heading back in there today. I'll get one."

"Thanks!" Christopher did a small leap into the air, nearly bumping Charlotte's nose with the top of his head.

"You're welcome. Now you better get back to practicing the stuff you do remember."

"Okay. You want to see some more?"

Charlotte planted her fists on her hips. "Sure. The more you practice, the better you'll be on the big day."

"Come on, Toby." Christopher hurried back to the first spot near the front porch where he had Toby sit. He thrust out his hand, palm forward. "Sit," he said again.

Toby sat.

Christopher again walked backward to the edge of the lawn. He signaled Toby with his hand. "Okay, come on, girl."

Toby trotted toward Christopher. When she was halfway there, Christopher signaled her again. Charlotte watched in amazement as Toby stopped and lay down. Yet she didn't fall over to her side as she typically did. Instead, her ears remained perked up and her eyes focused on Christopher.

Charlotte clapped. "Christopher, that's amazing!"

Hearing Charlotte's voice, Toby moved to a sitting position and cocked her head in Charlotte's direction. Charlotte covered her mouth with her hand. "Sorry about that."

"Toby." Christopher frowned. His voice was stern. Toby returned to the lying-down position. Christopher waited, and Toby waited too.

"Charlotte," Bob called from the barn.

She turned and waved at him, "Be there in a minute."

"Okay. Toby." Christopher motioned to her, and she trotted the rest of the way to Christopher, sitting just in front of his feet.

"Good job, Christopher." Charlotte clapped. Then she turned and started walking to the barn to see what Bob wanted.

"Wait, there's more!" Christopher called from behind her.

"I'm sure there is, but I need to go see what Grandpa wants. Why don't you show me the rest tonight?"

"Okay."

Charlotte didn't have to turn to know that Christopher was disappointed. She could hear it in his voice. He had been working so hard. Still, Bob needed her.

She imagined there was a lot he wanted to get done before the video people arrived.

She strode over to Bob's truck, where he was loading hay bales in the back. His neck strained, and his face flushed red as he lifted them. Charlotte thought about suggesting that Bob get Pete or Sam to help, but she bit her tongue. Bob was sensitive about getting too much "mothering" from his wife. Instead, she approached and leaned against the truck.

"You called?"

"Yeah," Bob panted as he loaded another bale. "Can you see if Sam's ready? He said he'd go into town and help me set up the Country Kitchen."

"He did?" Charlotte grabbed the end of the hay bale he was carrying and helped to ease it into the truck.

"Did you tell him about the video crew coming?" Charlotte asked.

"Didn't have to. He heard me talking to that Will guy on the phone this morning."

"And you're still okay with the video crew coming? I mean, fair week is as busy as they come."

"Well, Will said they'd be in and out in three or four days. Said they wouldn't touch my stuff and that he would drop off a check today. So I suppose I'm okay with it."

Charlotte turned away, hoping Bob didn't read the questions in her gaze. "Sure, I'll go check on Sam. He should be ready."

But am I? Am I ready for what this week holds?

EMILY WATCHED OUT THE WINDOW of Mel's Place, looking for her uncle's old truck. In the booth next to her sat her camera bag and camera. She'd taken a few more photos at Ashley's house last night, but not too many. Grandpa was right. Taking photos on this camera wasn't like taking them on her cell phone, where she could see them right away and just delete the ones she didn't like. Now, with each photo she took using the camera, she found herself keeping track of how much it would cost to develop the photo and eventually to replace the film.

Still, she was excited to see how they all turned out. Especially the ones she'd taken with Uncle Pete on the farm.

"How do you like the coffee?" Ashley called from behind the counter.

"It's good." Emily took another sip and smiled. It was a bit too sweet, but she didn't want to tell Ashley that. Ashley was training to be a barista, which was just a fancy word for the person who makes the espresso drinks.

"Do you want a cinnamon roll to go with it?" Ashley walked around the counter and waved her hand in front of the glass display, reminding Emily of the Vanna White lady and her *Wheel of Fortune* letters that Grandpa always watched on TV.

"Nah, I'm still stuffed from breakfast."

One thing Emily liked about staying at Ashley's house was that Ashley's mom often tried new recipes on them. Emily had especially liked the carrot muffins served up this morning. They were supposed to be healthy, but they tasted like a moist cupcake. Emily had liked them so much she'd eaten three of them *and* a smoothie. Add the coffee to that, and she was sugared out.

Emily saw Uncle Pete's truck rumbling down Lincoln Street; heard it too. Emily rose, grabbed her camera bag, and waved to Ashley. "Have fun working. I'll call you about meeting up at the fair later in the week."

"You got it," Ashley called, glancing over her shoulder as she set to work making a latte for a customer.

Emily hurried outside and jumped in Pete's truck.

"Hey, Uncle Pete. Thanks for picking me up."

"No problem." Her uncle offered her a smile, but Emily could see from his gaze and the set of his chin that something was wrong.

"Did something happen?"

"What do you mean?" Pete merged back into the traffic on Lincoln Street.

"On the farm? Did I miss something while I was gone?"

"Well, pretty much if you're gone for a few hours you'll miss something, but I'll let your grandparents fill you in. I don't want to get in the middle of it."

"Oh." Emily raised one eyebrow, noticing how Pete had said *your grandparents*. At first she worried that something had happened—maybe to a family member. But from the look on Uncle Pete's face, he was more ticked than sad. It most likely had something to do with Sam, or maybe an argument Pete had had with Grandpa. Those were the things that seemed to bother Uncle Pete the most.

"Thanks for taking me to pick up my photos."

"No problem. I'm kind of anxious to see how they turned out."

They pulled up to Kepler's Pharmacy and walked in matching strides to the photo-developing counter in the back of the store. Two other kids her age were already in line; Emily recognized them as 4-H kids.

Finally it was Emily's turn. She smiled at the lady across the counter, whose nametag read NORA.

"Emily Slater. I should have some photos ready."

"Oh, yeah. Slater." The lady turned and grabbed an envelope from the top of the stack. Then she punched some buttons on the register. "That will be seventy-four cents."

"Seventy-four cents?" Emily turned to her uncle and smiled. "That's cheaper than I thought."

"Actually, there were only three that turned out. The rest were too dark so we didn't charge for those."

Emily felt her smile fade. She felt her uncle's hand on her shoulder. "It's okay for a first try. Don't worry about it. Maybe we can head home, take some more photos, and try again." He picked up a pamphlet on the counter that talked about light settings and film. "I was so worried about showing you how to frame shots I didn't think about checking all the light settings." He pushed back his ball cap and scratched his head. "Man, it's like a decade ago since I used a camera."

Emily shook her head. "It's okay. We don't have to worry about it. Even if we get some shots we don't have time to develop them. The entries for the fair need to be turned in tomorrow, and they need to be framed and stuff."

Pete squared his shoulders. "Are you giving up that quick?" He eyed her. "I thought you had more guts than that."

"I do have guts." Emily jutted out her chin.

"Uh, we do have one-hour developing," the lady, Nora, butted in. For the first time Emily realized the clerk was still waiting for her seventy-four cents.

She quickly pulled out her money and paid.

"Still, Uncle Pete, we don't have time to drive all the way back to the farm and take photos. I just—"

"Then how about we head over to the fairgrounds? There are some pretty places near the flower garden. Or you can take photos of the carnies setting up the rides." He winked at her.

"Okay, I guess. If you're not going to leave me alone about it. But if these shots don't turn out, I'll just plan on having no entries this year."

✒ Chapter
Seven

S am grabbed the twine wrapped around the hay bale
and tugged, lifting it from the back of his grandfather's truck. Yesterday he'd honestly regretted inviting Jordan. Really. What would his friend think of the
fair . . . the people of Bedford . . . the farm?

"Over there, against the wall," his grandmother's friend
Hannah commented, following him with a broom and
sweeping up the pieces of hay that fell from the bales.
Hannah's hair was tied up in a scarf, and she was wearing
paint-splattered jeans that showed she was here to work. In
fact, she didn't seem fazed by the fact that she wore no
makeup and her hair stuck our from under her scarf every
which way.

Looking around, Sam noticed everyone was the same.
Their clothes were well-worn and comfortable. In fact, it
was those "outsiders in fancy clothes" that they had a hard
time trusting.

In San Diego things had been different. People dressed
up to go to the store or to attend their kids' basketball
games. He and Jordan hadn't been into clothes, but they
hadn't worn stuff from the Salvation Army either. They'd

spent their time skateboarding and talking to girls at the beach. They'd bodysurfed and hung out at the mall. They'd pretty much done whatever they wanted as long as they didn't get in trouble and weren't out too late.

Everything was different in Nebraska. Farm life was different. The last thing he'd wanted was for Jordan to make fun of his Uncle Pete's truck or laugh at the rodeo. Back in San Diego they used to laugh at guys dressed up as cowboys and farmers, and in Nebraska you got noticed if you didn't dress that way.

Sam carried the bale across the fair's Country Kitchen dining area and lined it up against the wall with the others. His hands itched from the hay, and he clapped them together, brushing off the dust as he hummed a Two Dead Brothers tune.

Sam was sort of excited about the idea of them shooting a music video on the farm, but he wondered what Jordan would think. He only wished it was another group, another singer.

"Amazing how quickly everything can change," he mumbled under his breath.

"Yeah, it is looking pretty nice in here, isn't it?" Hannah commented, obviously thinking Sam was talking to her.

"Uh, yes, ma'am."

"It's awfully nice of you to come and help, Sam," Hannah added.

"No problem. My friend's flight isn't coming in until this afternoon, so I didn't have much to do this morning."

She leaned on her broom. "Perfect time for Jimmy to come in—fair's always fun for young folks."

"It's Jordan," Sam corrected.

"Oh yes. I knew it started with a J. Perfect time for him to come. It should be the most exciting week ever."

Sam didn't know if she was talking about the fair or the video shoot, so he just nodded. Actually, he didn't know if Hannah even knew about the video shoot, but if she didn't he was sure it was just a matter of time. Grandma seemed to talk to her about everything.

"I hope so," Sam said, and then he hurried back to the truck to unload another bale.

"Hey, Sam." He was surprised to see his sister walking down the roadway with Uncle Pete.

"What are you up to?" As soon as Sam saw Emily he knew he should tell her about the music video—about how Shae Lynne was going to be on their farm. But just the idea caused a knot in his stomach to tighten. If he told Emily she'd go crazy with excitement and would make a scene, and his nerves couldn't handle that right now.

"Oh, I'm just going to try one more time to take some good photos." She tucked her hair behind her ear. "The last ones didn't turn out so great."

Sam caught Pete's gaze and could tell from the look on Pete's face that he hadn't spilled the beans to Emily yet.

Instead of saying anything Pete unfolded a brochure he was carrying in his hands and began to study it.

"Yeah, well, there are some cute baby animals over in the animal barns." Sam glanced around, his eye catching on the flower garden. "And those sunflowers are nice—almost as nice as the ones Grandma planted."

"Yeah, we're going to figure out these settings, and then

we're going to walk around and check things out." Emily took two steps and paused, turning back to Sam. "Hey, today's the day you're going up to get Jordan. How cool is that?"

"Very cool," Sam mumbled, wiping the sweat from his forehead. It was only 10:00 AM and the sun beating down was already unbearable. He eyed the people hurrying around him, gearing up for the big event. "I'm, uh, sure Jordan is going to think this place is, uh, something unlike anything he's ever seen."

He pulled his cell phone from his pocket and checked the time. It was nearly time to head to Omaha. For the strangest reason, hanging around and unloading hay bales almost seemed more appealing.

"ONE-HOUR DEVELOPING, PLEASE." Emily set two rolls of film on the counter and then drummed her fingers, feeling the tension in her shoulders. With Uncle Pete's help, she'd figured out the right light setting, yet she worried that there was something else she'd done wrong.

"One hour? Sure. Do you need any special sizes or anything—eight-by-tens that you want to frame?" the woman asked.

Emily forced a smile. Didn't this lady, Nora, remember that she was the same one who'd just been in here earlier today with a roll of dark photos that weren't worth developing? Emily didn't know if she was being sarcastic or not. "I might, after I see them. I need to make sure they turn out first."

Nora nodded, and gave Emily the receipt from the photo

envelope. Then she handed the film to the guy working in the back.

"Okay, thanks. See you in an hour." Emily turned to go.

Pete placed a hand on Emily's shoulder. "Sweet. That gives us time to head over to the tractor supply."

"Gee, that's just how I want to spend my day."

"You know you love it," Pete said, softly slugging Emily's shoulder with his knuckle. "In fact—"

"Hey, Emily!" Emily turned to see her friend Hunter coming toward them.

"Hey, Hunter," Emily replied.

"Is it true they're filming a Shae Lynne video at your farm?" Hunter gushed.

"Music video?" Emily glanced up at her uncle. "A music video with Shae Lynne? Are you serious?"

Pete placed a finger to his lips, shushing her. "Not too loud. We're not supposed to tell too many people because we don't want the farm swarming with—"

"Uncle Pete, is *this* what you've been holding back from telling me?" Every bit of anger was replaced by a surge of excitement. Emily tugged on her uncle's arm and led him outside. Hunter followed. "There's gonna be a music video shot on *our* farm with, like, the best country music singer ever?"

"Well, since it's obviously not a secret anymore, yes. But Grandma and Grandpa will have to give you the details, because as far as I'm concerned this thing is going to blow up, just like it's doing now."

"A music video at our house." Emily turned to Hunter and tucked the photo receipt in her pocket, almost not caring about her pictures anymore.

"So how did you know about this before I did?" Emily asked Hunter.

"Well, my dad and I heard some guys talking at the feed store. I'm glad I ran into you. It's cool about the video and all, but I wanted to make sure you were coming to watch me in the barrel races Wednesday night."

"Uh, sure. Ashley and I are definitely planning on being there," Emily assured her friend.

"Okay, great. I gotta go help my dad, but I'll see you then," Hunter said and hurried down the street.

Emily turned to Uncle Pete, who by this time was heading toward his truck.

"Do we have to go to the tractor supply? Can't we just go home? I want to hear all about the video."

"Nope. I have stuff I need to get. Then we're going to come back here and look at your photos." Pete crossed his arms over his chest. "We're not going to let some Nashville bigwig interrupt our life. The priority this week will be the fair and our usual chores. I'm sticking to that."

AN HOUR LATER, Emily's fingers hurriedly opened the envelope and slid out the photos, placing them on the counter. She chuckled at the one of Ashley sticking out her tongue. There was another one of a bird outside Ashley's bedroom window that was blurry, but the ones she'd taken at the fairgrounds . . .

Emily's eyes widened when she saw them. "Look, Uncle Pete."

Her uncle peered over her shoulder, but he didn't say anything.

"Uncle Pete?" She turned to see his jaw had dropped in amazement.

"Wow," he finally mumbled. "Wow."

Emily lifted one of the photographs of a baby goat for him to see better, and her chest warmed with pride. There was another shot she'd taken of one of the show horses that had been warming up in a corral. In the photo, the beautiful mare was trotting, with her long mane and tail flowing as she moved. Above her, the sky was bright blue, and the fair barns in the distance looked charming and rustic.

In the next photo a large steer stood poised, peering down at a dog that had been wandering through the barns. The dog was looking up, head cocked, and from the look on the dog's face it appeared as if the steer were in the middle of telling the dog an enchanting story.

"Man, it looks like these could be photos from a calendar or something. They turned out really good." Pete studied a close-up photograph of a sunflower in the fairgrounds garden.

"Yeah. They're even better than I expected," Emily said. "I think we got the settings right."

"Oh, I think the settings are only part of it." Pete patted her shoulder. "You have a great eye, Em."

Emily's fingers trailed over the edges of another of the sunflower photos; she couldn't believe she'd actually taken it.

Pete motioned to the young woman behind the counter. She had short, spiky hair and an attitude that seemed equally as sharp. "Ma'am, how much would it cost to get these enlarged?"

She was busy flipping through a large pile of photo

envelopes and didn't bother to look up. "It's $5.99 a photo, and they'll be ready Wednesday."

"Okay, how much would they cost if I want them tomorrow?"

"Sorry." The young woman chomped on her gum. "We have a pile of orders, and we can't get them done before then."

"Are you serious?" A wave of disappointment washed over Emily. Tears sprang to her eyes.

"Wednesday?" Pete mumbled something that Emily couldn't make out. "That's not going to work. We need them tomorrow."

The lady shrugged and then turned back to the photo-developing machine. "Sorry."

"Oh well, I guess we can try again next year." Emily shrugged, trying to act like it didn't bother her. Still, her throat felt tight and thick. She returned the photographs to the envelope.

"Is there someone else I can talk to? A manager or something?" Pete leaned forward on the counter.

Hearing this, an older gentleman with a white moustache and bright blue eyes stepped out from behind the machine in the back. "Can I help you?"

"We were hoping to get some enlargements by tomorrow."

The man turned his attention from Pete to Emily. "Are you the young lady who took these photos?"

"Uh, yeah."

"Those were great. Very nice composition."

"Thanks. I like them too."

"My niece was going to try to enter them in the fair, but

they have to be entered tomorrow," Pete explained. "This is her first time entering stuff because she just moved here last year from California, and, well, it's a long story, but she was really hoping to get them enlarged."

The older man looked around, checking to see if anyone else was in hearing distance. Then he pushed his glasses up on his nose, leaned forward, and lowered his voice. "Well, I'm not supposed to do this, but I can stay a little longer tonight and work on them. I've seen a lot of entries come through here, and I think it would be a shame if you missed entering photos this nice."

"Really?" Emily clapped her hands in front of her. "Are you serious?"

"Sure. I especially like the one with the steer and dog. I'm thinking you should do a larger size than eight-by-ten though . . ." The man continued on, turning and talking to Uncle Pete about sizes and finishes on the photographs.

Emily tried to follow all his technical terms, but her mind was fixed on the fair. She smiled as she imagined thousands of people walking by and seeing her photos on display. More than that, she wondered if Shae Lynne would see them and ask Emily for copies.

Uncle Pete tapped Emily's hand. "After church would work, right?"

"Uh, what? Sorry. I was daydreaming."

"I was just saying that we can pick the photos up tomorrow after church."

"Oh, yeah, sure. That would be great. Thank you." Emily glanced into the man's kind eyes, wondering if someone in San Diego would have bent the rules to help her like this. She doubted it. "Thank you so much, sir."

Emily wasn't sure if her feet touched the ground as they walked toward the front of the pharmacy for the second time that day. Also for the second time, they heard a voice calling to them.

"Pete! Emily!"

Emily glanced up to see Dana Simons approaching.

"Dana!" Pete hurried forward. A grin filled his face.

"Hi, Miss Simons." Emily waved.

Dana tried to act casual, but Emily could see her face glowed from seeing Pete.

"Hey, Pete, I'm glad I ran into you." Dana leaned forward and placed a kiss on his cheek.

Pete held her close in a hug, seemingly reluctant to release her. "So you're back?"

Heat rose to Dana's cheeks as she stepped back from his embrace. She tried to be nonchalant as she tucked her dark hair behind her ear. "Yep, the teacher training ended yesterday, and I drove back last night." She turned to Emily. "See? Even teachers have to go to school."

"Do you need a hall pass to go to the bathroom too?" Emily laughed at her own joke.

Dana smirked. "Thankfully not. The rules are a lot more lax."

"Well, I'm glad you made it back." Pete took her hand in his. "That's a long drive."

"Not too bad, except for the fact that the radio in my car was broken, which meant I just had more time to think." She winked at Pete and lowered her voice. "Mostly about us."

Pete's grin widened, if that were at all possible. Emily turned and pretended she was interested in the rack of magazines, letting Pete and Dana have a minute of semiprivacy. She glanced at the headlines but didn't really read them. After all, they were the same old stuff—movie stars having babies, getting married, breaking up.

"Well, I'd love to hear about your trip and classes. How about we have dinner soon? Maybe I'll even cook."

"You'd cook for me?" The excitement in Dana's voice made Emily smile.

"Of course. Can't guarantee it will be edible, but for you I'd try."

They continued talking about the teacher training, the farm, and the fair. Emily noticed Pete didn't say anything about the video. It was as if he hoped that by not talking about it, it would go away.

Not wanting to interrupt, Emily picked up one of the gossip magazines and flipped through the pages. Her heartbeat quickened as she saw an interview with Shae Lynne. Emily still found it hard to believe she'd actually meet this famous person soon. She looked at the photos of Shae Lynne at the CMT awards, at her Nashville mansion, on her bus.

"Ready, Em?" Pete asked.

Emily thought about telling Pete she wanted to buy the magazine, but she changed her mind when she saw the caption under one of the photos. It was a picture of Shae Lynne sitting on a porch swing. The caption read, "I'm just looking for a simple man—a farmer or cowboy to sweep me off my feet. That's the type of person I've always imagined myself marrying."

"Yeah, I'm ready to go." Emily turned and eyed her uncle, as if seeing him from an outsider's point of view:

tall, thin, and, she supposed, handsome. And rugged. Someone could tell just by looking at him that Uncle Pete worked hard for a living.

What if Uncle Pete and Shae Lynne started dating? After all, if Pete and Dana were serious you'd think they'd have done something about it by now. What if . . . Emily pushed that thought out of her mind. She liked Miss Simons; she really did.

Emily closed the magazine and put it back on the rack. Then she followed Pete and Dana as they walked to his truck. Still, she couldn't completely forget the idea of her uncle falling in love with a famous country singer. Or rather her falling in love with him.

What if someone like Uncle Pete *was* who Shae Lynne was looking for? *It wouldn't be too bad to have someone famous in our family.*

But as Dana and Uncle Pete gave each other a good-bye hug, Emily felt a little guilt for even thinking those thoughts. Still, another part of her had the smallest hope that it could happen.

After all, it was Shae Lynne . . .

Chapter Eight

Sam pulled over in the fast-food restaurant's parking lot and looked at the map one more time. He'd been driving for over three hours without any problems so far. Just a few more miles, and he'd be at the airport. Right on time to pick up Jordan.

"What was the name of the street I turn off on again?" Sam mumbled to himself. Even though he'd officially driven almost this far when he'd tried to run away to Colorado in February, it seemed strange to him that his grandparents had let him go this far without them. After all, he was only seventeen. What would happen if his old car broke down? Or if he'd gotten lost and missed picking Jordan up?

Last time he'd driven to Omaha he'd been with his Grandpa. It was Christmastime, and he'd been planning to fly to California to visit Jordan. The vacation to San Diego hadn't worked out due to the weather; his trip was canceled. Now he was excited to see his friend again, but he wished it had been on his home turf. Too many things about Jordan coming to Nebraska freaked him out.

"You'll do fine driving up there by yourself," his grandpa had said, patting him on the back at the breakfast table. "It's good for you to get out and spread your wings. You never know; next year you might be going off to college somewhere."

Sam didn't know if their insistence that he pick up Jordan alone had more to do with them wanting him to become responsible, or with their just being too busy to join him. He guessed it was a little of both. Though he tried at times to act like he was invincible, he had to admit that most of the time growing up and doing new things scared him. Maybe it was the responsibility part. But he couldn't let anyone know that. Not his grandparents. And definitely not Jordan.

Sam soon found the street he needed, and a few minutes later he was in the airport parking lot. He got out of his car and followed the signs to baggage claim.

He'd only been waiting around five minutes when he heard someone shouting his name. Sam recognized the voice before he recognized his friend. Jordan had grown at least six inches and now towered over Sam.

"Hey, short stuff," Jordan called. "Give me five."

Sam lifted his hand and Jordan slapped it. Then, to Sam's surprise, Jordan gave him a big hug.

"Dude, look at you," Sam said.

"I know. I know. My dad has been complaining like crazy. My parents can't seem to keep food in the house." Jordan laughed. "I hope your grandma is prepared."

"Oh yeah, no problem. She's the best cook ever, and she cooks enough to feed an army."

"Sounds like my type of place. I might not ever want to go home."

As they waited for Jordan's suitcase, they talked about the flight and their friends back in Southern California. Then, once they had Jordan's luggage, they strode out to Sam's car.

"This car is yours? Sweet." Jordan tossed his suitcase in the trunk and his backpack in the backseat, and then climbed into the front seat.

"Yeah, my Uncle Pete got it for me."

"He sounds pretty cool, man."

"Yeah, Pete's cool. In fact, most of my family is, now that I'm used to being here."

"So what are our plans for the week? Are we going on a cattle drive, or maybe breaking some wild horses?"

Sam paused, again wondering if he should tell Jordan about the music video or if he should wait. After all, neither of them liked country music, so there was no rush to share this information.

"Well." Sam started the car and drove out of the airport parking lot, paying his buck at the toll booth. "The fair starts Tuesday, but we don't have to go if you don't want to."

"The county fair? Like in *Charlotte's Web*?"

Sam laughed. "Yeah, sort of. Only not quite as animated."

Jordan laughed, getting the joke. "Well, that's cool. I've always wanted to go to a real county fair."

"You have? I thought you'd rather just hang out and skateboard. We don't have any skate parks or anything but—"

Jordan waved his hand in the air. "Dude, I've been working so much that I'm a little rusty on my board. Besides, I can skate anywhere, but how often do I get to experience a fair?" Jordan sat up straighter. "Will there be any cute girls there?"

"Yeah, my girlfriend is real cute, but she's not available. But some of her friends are all right."

Jordan raised his hands, surrendering. "That's all you have to say. I'm there."

Sam laughed. It was great being with Jordan again, picking up where they'd left off as if only a week had passed, not a year and a half.

Sam pulled into the closest hamburger joint, deciding they had better get some food before driving home. Then maybe he'd tell Jordan about Shae Lynne.

Sam parked and turned off his car, but before he climbed out, Jordan's laughter filled the car.

"No way! You can't be serious." Jordan pointed to two teens about their age, parking a hay truck in the back corner. The guys climbed out and strode to the restaurant. Their faces were smudged with dirt, and their hands were tucked into the deep pockets of their overalls. If Jordan hadn't pointed them out Sam wouldn't have thought anything about them. In Nebraska life meant work. And work meant, well, getting dirty and wearing clothes that fit the job.

"Yeah, I know. My Uncle Pete looks like that all the time. I wouldn't be caught dead hanging around town looking like that."

"Dude, where did they escape from, the funny farm?" Jordan slapped his leg.

Sam laughed. "Nah, most likely just got off the back forty."

"Doing what? Rolling around with their farm animals?"

Sam's smile slid from his face when Jordan's laughter didn't let up. "No. They've been working. You know, riding their tractors and—"

"Their *tractors*?" Jordan said the word with disbelief, as if Sam had just told him they'd been riding camels. "No way, Sam! Where's my camera? I need a photo of those tractor boys." Jordan turned and pulled his backpack from the backseat.

Before he could unzip the pocket, Sam reached over and touched Jordan's hand. "Hey, I don't think you should do that." Sam didn't want to tell Jordan that he often drove a tractor. Jordan had no idea what kind of work these guys did every day. No idea what kind of work *he* did. Or Grandpa. Or Uncle Pete. "Seriously, you just need to keep your camera where it is."

Jordan was still laughing, but his laughter softened, and he looked at Sam in surprise. "What? Are you kidding? Our friends back home are going to die when they see these hicks."

Jordan unzipped his backpack and pulled out a digital camera.

"Man, I'm serious." Sam's voice was stern, and it obviously caught Jordan by surprise because Jordan's laughter finally stopped, and he turned to Sam with wide eyes.

"Sam, man, don't get offended. It's not like I'm making fun of *you* or anything."

"I know. It's just that things are different around here. When I moved here I thought it was all lame too, but then I realized it's no joke. Not many people have an easy life around here. They work hard."

"I wasn't saying they don't work hard. It's just like between here and the airport I've already seen more tractors, farmers, and cows than I've seen in my lifetime. It's like I've been transported back to 1850 or something."

"Yeah, well, you better be thankful for those things." Sam pointed at the hamburger place in front of him. "Where do you think all the food you eat comes from? Do you think it just magically appears on the supermarket shelves?"

Jordan shook his head and closed the car door. "Man, Sam, what's gotten into you? I was just messing around."

Jordan stalked into the restaurant and ordered, paying for his food himself without waiting for Sam. Sam followed, ordering his favorite meal, but by the time he sat down with it he wasn't that hungry anymore. He felt annoyed with Jordan, but also upset with himself.

What had gotten into him? What was his problem? Having Jordan here was supposed to be fun.

Sam pushed his soda aside, and glanced at the guy sitting across from him. That guy used to be his best friend.

Sam sighed, knowing it was going to be a long three hours back to Bedford.

ON SATURDAY AFTERNOON Charlotte sat at the dining table, looking over the fair schedule for the week ahead and penciling in where she needed to be when. Christopher sat on one side of her, reading over the new dog-training manual she'd picked up after safely dropping off the new batch of pies at Rosemary's house. Emily sat on the other side of her, looking over the photographs she'd taken and occasionally asking questions about the video shoot.

Christopher glanced up from the manual. "Grandma, when are Sam and Jordan supposed to be here? I've been waiting forever," he whined.

"Forever?" Emily sighed. "You love to exaggerate."

"Okay, not forever, but for as long as I knew Jordan was coming. I like him. He always gives me shoulder rides."

Emily glanced up from her photographs. "Yeah, well, you were a lot smaller then. You're too big now."

"No sir. Maybe Jordan got bigger too. You ever think of that?"

"Unfortunately," Charlotte interrupted, "Sam called from the road to say he and Jordan were going to stop and hang out and skate around the high school for a while."

"What?" Christopher folded his arms over his chest. "That's not fair. Doesn't he know we've been waiting?"

"Yes, but, well, I'm sure they just want to spend time together, to catch up before Jordan has to come and meet everyone."

Even though Charlotte believed that, she also guessed something else was going on. When she'd talked to Sam she couldn't help but notice the discouragement in his voice. She had a sneaky feeling he was trying to find stuff to do around town to stall before coming home to the farm.

Charlotte bit her lip, remembering the first days and weeks when her grandchildren had arrived. Would Jordan have the same shocked and dismayed attitude when he arrived here? She hadn't really thought about that, and she hoped it wouldn't be the case.

"Did the video guy tell you what day they're going to be here?" Emily's voice interrupted Charlotte's thoughts. She glanced over to see her granddaughter pushing the photos to the side and opening a bottle of nail polish she'd brought down from her room.

"Actually I think they might be coming out today. He's going to get back to us." Charlotte wrinkled her nose at the strong odor of polish.

"I do have to turn my back on Toby after I get her to sit," Christopher interjected.

"Uh-huh," Charlotte answered, writing down the time when the dog show would be happening.

"So do you think they're going to need extras in the video?" Emily asked, leaning close to the table as she worked on her nails.

The phone rang, and Bob rose to answer it. "Hello. Yes, this is Bob." He was quiet, listening. "Sure, that's fine. Yes."

He leaned against the counter and picked at the grapes Charlotte had set out, popping them into his mouth as he talked. "Okay. Yes, I'll let my wife know."

Charlotte watched Bob as she chatted with the kids, noticing the ease on his face.

"Great. Talk to you later. Bye now." Bob hung up the phone and walked to the dining room with lightness in his step. Everyone's eyes were on him as he approached.

"So Will and the set designer will be here in an hour or so. They're just getting something to eat in town. They're going to scope out the farm, figure out where they want to do their shots, and check out the animals.

"The animals?" Charlotte frowned.

Bob chuckled. "For props, or something. I guess they want to see how our cows, chickens, and pets look in case they want to bring fill-ins."

"Are you joking?" Emily shook her fingers to dry her nail polish. "What if Trudy doesn't cut it? They're going to bring in a fill-in cow to take her place?"

"Our cow is going to have a body double?" Charlotte laughed.

"Can I show them the chickens?" Christopher jumped to his feet.

"I think we all can." Bob approached the window and looked out.

"Did they say anything about extras?" Emily asked again.

"Yes, actually they did. But I don't have any details yet."

Emily smiled and went back to painting her nails with precision, as if prepping herself to step in as needed, humming a tune Charlotte came to recognize as Shae Lynne's song "Just Another Friday."

As Bob walked outside, Charlotte was sure she could feel the load lighten. They would be able to build up their nest egg. She imagined that took a ton of bricks off Bob's shoulders. Charlotte just wished she could feel so at ease about the decision.

If they're worried about the chickens being good enough, what about us? What if they change their minds? Are we depending on too much too soon?

THE PHONE RANG just as Charlotte was checking the pantry to see what they'd have for dinner, and Bob answered it again. Expectant eyes focused on him as he returned to the table.

"It was Frank down at the fairgrounds. They need to write a few checks and want me to come down. They need two signers on each check, and Chet is up in Harding."

"But what about those video guys?" Charlotte looked up at Bob. "You're not going to leave me here to deal with them, are you?"

"You don't have to deal with them, Charlotte. You just have to show them around. The kids will help you."

Charlotte narrowed her gaze at Bob. While it was true that this money would be a blessing to their bank account, she still worried about the video's potentially negative influence on the kids.

She decided on roast chicken and potatoes for dinner while Christopher and Emily waited on the porch, discussing who should show what. Charlotte could hear them through the open window and was happy when they finally decided they would go together to give a tour of the farm.

Soon a black sedan pulled into the driveway. Welcomed by a barking and excited Toby, Will got out of the car and approached the porch, introducing his co-worker, Buck. This time Will was dressed in an ordinary pair of black jeans and a white T-shirt. Charlotte was happy to see he'd given up on the brightly colored vest and cowboy hat from yesterday.

"Mrs. Stevenson." Will scanned the farm. "It's even more beautiful than I remember. Don't you think so, Buck?"

"Absolutely. This is even better than I was picturing. It's like the Waltons meet the twenty-first century."

"The who?" Christopher asked, scratching his head.

"Oh, just an old television show your mom and uncles used to watch," Charlotte explained. "It's about a big family that lived in the country."

"Did they have a cow like Trudy?" Christopher asked.

"I'm not sure." Will nodded his chin toward the barn. "Why don't you show me, and we'll find out."

The tour took longer than Charlotte thought it should. Every few steps the set designer stopped to write some notes and take a few photographs.

"We have to choose the best spots and try to film as much as we can," Buck explained. "There's a lot of equipment to set up, and we want to move it as few times as possible."

In the barn, it was Emily who took the lead in introducing their cow.

"This is Trudy. She's a Holstein, and she provides the milk for the farm. We brought her in early from grazing. She usually stays out until dark," Emily explained. "It takes about twenty minutes to milk her by hand." She patted the cow's back.

"You actually drink milk after it comes out of that?" Buck eyed the cow.

"Don't you drink milk?" Charlotte asked, trying to hide her grin.

"Yes, but only in lattes or those gallon containers I get from the supermarket shelf." Buck rolled his eyes; suddenly he didn't seem as friendly as he had been when they first met.

"Do you want me to show you how to milk her?" Emily asked with a smirk. "Then you'll know exactly what you're drinking."

Will shook his head. "Don't think we'll need that. We just need her to stand in the field during one segment of the video. No milking involved. But we *would* like to see your horses."

"I'll show you." Emily led the way to the corral. The sun was lower now but still warmed the farm.

"The black one is Shania. The bay with the blaze on his face is Tom. Ben is the other bay with the star on his forehead," Emily explained, pointing.

"Yeah, Princess is the one we ride," Christopher cut in. "And Stormy is Britney's baby," he recited with pride. "The horses belong to Uncle Pete."

Charlotte stood in the back of the group, watching as the two men looked at the horses and the farm with a critical eye. For the first time it became real to her that their farm was going to be featured in a video that thousands, maybe millions, of people would watch. It was an overwhelming thought, really, that their place had been chosen for its rustic charm and quaintness. To her, *rustic* just meant they hadn't been as diligent at repainting the house and barn as they should have been. And *quaint* . . . well, it was a nice way to say that things were old.

The more the men walked and talked, the more they seemed to relax. They exclaimed over the horses in the corral, the tall stalks of corn, and the rows of soybeans. Walking back to the house, they even eyed Charlotte's garden with its tall sunflowers.

"We could show you the creek too." Charlotte pointed to the line of trees in the distance. "That's what the farm's named after, Heather Creek."

"Oh, I'm sure it's beautiful, Mrs. Stevenson, but we couldn't get our crew down there without tearing up a lot of your crops and land. We'll have to stick to shooting around the house and barn this time," Will explained.

"That's fine, but please call me Charlotte. And I'm sorry I've been so rude; I haven't been very hospitable. It's hot out here. Would you like something to drink? Water, juice, milk?" She couldn't help but smile as she said that last word.

"A bottle of water would be great," Buck commented.

"I'll take one of those too," Will said. "That's kind of you."

"We don't have bottled water, but it's cold from our well." Emily offered a huge grin as if she were trying out for a toothpaste commercial. "Would you like water in glasses? Or maybe lemonade?"

"Either would be great, thank you." Will eased himself down onto the front porch steps. Buck reluctantly sat beside him. Charlotte could picture him in some nice studio, but he seemed very uncomfortable on the farm.

Emily hurried into the house to get the water, and Will whistled to Toby.

"What's your dog's name again?"

"Toby. It's a she. You want to see her tricks?" Christopher asked, tugging on Buck's arm.

Buck pulled his arm back. Then he leaned close to Christopher and talked low. "Hey, kid, I'm here to shoot a music video, not an episode of Toby the Wonder Dog. Why don't you two go run off and chase the chickens or something?"

Charlotte turned and eyed the man, letting him know she'd heard his remark. Then she focused her attention on Christopher.

"Maybe our guests will be interested a little later. I was just going to ask if they wanted some pie."

"Pie? Homemade pie?" For the first time Charlotte noticed a smile on Buck's face.

"Yes, we have peach, strawberry, and apple-caramel."

"Yeah, we have a lot of different kinds because Grandma was driving them into town when a lamb ran in front of the car. She slammed on the brakes, and the pies got smashed, so now we get to eat them."

"Smashed?" Will cocked an eyebrow.

Charlotte chuckled. "They just hit each other, and the crusts got a little crumbled. They still taste great, I promise."

The men seemed more relaxed when Charlotte and Emily returned with the water and dessert. Buck had chosen strawberry, and Will had picked apple-caramel.

Will closed his eyes as he took a bite. He chewed slowly, savoring it. A smile filled his face as he swallowed. "I have to say, Charlotte, this is the best pie I've ever eaten. You should go into business. You could be the next Sara Lee or Little Debbie."

Charlotte and Emily looked at each other and laughed.

"Oh, we've done that," Christopher commented. "It was called the Heather Creek Pie Company, right, Grandma?"

"That's right." Then Charlotte went on to explain about their venture.

Interestingly enough, the men seemed to enjoy hearing about the pie company. They finished their pies and began asking more questions about living in Nebraska. Soon the kids were telling them about the tornado and the tractor accident.

As they talked, the two men also shared stories about their work on music videos—about the places they'd visited, and some of the people they'd worked with.

"Shae Lynne is a dream client," Will said. "She's new enough to still listen to direction, yet talented enough to blow us away with her ideas and input."

"We're looking forward to meeting her." Charlotte gathered the plates and forks.

"Yeah, and I have a feeling she'll like it here," Buck commented, glancing around again. "In fact, she may not want to leave."

Charlotte noticed Will sketching in a notebook as they talked.

"May I ask what you're doing?" She leaned in for a better look.

"Oh, I'm creating a shot list for the video. I'm thinking about the composition of the shots I want, and then Buck will know how to set up the cameras."

Emily's face lit up. "Composition? I'm learning about that. Do you use the law of thirds?"

"Yes, I do, actually. See?" Will showed Emily the sketch, pointing with his pencil. "Picture Shae Lynne singing in front of the sunflowers. One-third of the shot will be her, one-third will be the flowers, and one-third will be the barn."

"Cool." Emily's face brightened. "I think that's going to be great!"

"So, what song are you going to be shooting?" Charlotte asked, proud of herself to be talking in their lingo.

"Oh, it's one off her new album that will be coming out at Christmas. The song is called 'Always and Forever with You.'" Will nodded toward the garden area. "This whole setting should be just right for the song."

"Well, I aim to please." Charlotte smiled.

She heard the sound of Pete's truck approaching even before she saw it. Toby ran out to greet him, and Pete seemed not at all pleased to see the black sedan parked in front of the house. He climbed out and looked as if he were headed to the barn when Charlotte waved to him.

"Pete!" She motioned him over.

Pete strode over wearing his work jeans, T-shirt and ball cap. As he approached, she saw the two men glance at each other.

"Pete, it's good to see you again." Will stood and shook Pete's hand. "And this is my friend Buck Anderson."

Pete nodded. "Buck."

"We were just telling stories about the farm." Christopher turned to Emily. "Remember that time someone was stealing vegetables from the garden?"

"Yeah, and we found out it was a homeless person. But we helped him out. He lives here in Bedford now," she explained to Will. "We see him at church sometimes."

The men acted like they were interested in the story, but for the most part Buck kept eyeing Pete.

Finally, when there was a break in the conversation, Buck stood and strode to Pete's side. "You know, for one of our shots we'd like to have a farmer in the field plowing."

Pete smirked. "Well, that will be difficult since we don't plow this time of year."

"Yes, well, plowing isn't the point. The point is the farmer on a tractor." Buck seemed irritated by Pete's attitude.

"My dad might be interested." Pete crossed his arms over his chest.

"Uh, that's not really what we were thinking. We want a younger guy. You know, someone like you."

Pete's eyes widened and his jaw grew slack. Then he cocked one eyebrow, as if to say, *You've got to be kidding*.

"Is the farmer on the tractor like a prop?" Christopher's eyes brightened. "Don't worry, Uncle Pete. Trudy's going to be a prop too. If she can do it, so can you."

Charlotte chuckled. "I don't think Pete is worried about *if* he can do it, Christopher. It's if he *wants* to."

"Why wouldn't you want to, Uncle Pete?" Christopher scratched his head.

"Well, I, uh . . ." Pete stammered.

Charlotte could tell he was looking for the right words without being rude in front of the kids.

"You know, we won't need more than a few hours of your time," Will insisted. "And we'd be willing to pay a third of what we offered to your parents."

"A third? You're joking, right?"

"No sir, I'm not."

Charlotte saw Pete's hard gaze soften.

"Surely you can help out, Pete. Right? You'd hate for them to have to find someone else around town . . ." Charlotte let her voice trail off.

"Well, I suppose if it's not going to take too long. I've

been wanting to do something special for Dana for a while, so I could use the money." Pete's eyes brightened.

"Something special?" Charlotte tried not to get too hopeful.

"Yes, and it's something I won't tell you about because I know how you are, Mom. You'd share it with one or two people, and pretty soon the whole town of Bedford would know."

Charlotte placed a hand on her hip and tried not to be offended. "Okay. I guess you don't have to tell me."

"So you'll do it?" Will asked Pete.

"Yes, sign me up." Pete locked eyes with Emily. "If people are going to be talking around town, I might as well give them something good to talk about."

Pete had just walked off with a twinkle in his eyes when another car pulled up. Charlotte noticed Bill, Anna, and the girls piling out from the car.

"Grandma!" the girls exclaimed as they hurried onto the porch.

"Mother," Anna said with her arms outstretched.

Charlotte gave her daughter-in-law a quick squeeze and couldn't help but pat Anna's round tummy. "This is the rest of our family, as if you haven't guessed," Charlotte explained to Will and Buck. "And we can't wait to meet the newest member."

Bill walked up too, but he wasn't wearing a smile like everyone else.

"Bill." Charlotte gave her son a one-armed hug. "Glad you could come. Would you like a piece of pie?"

"No thanks. Actually I've come to read the contract Dad's going to sign."

"The contract?" Charlotte patted his arm. "I thought you came for a visit."

"It's my job, Mom. I want to see exactly what this video thing entails. It sounds like serious business."

"Serious?" Charlotte glanced toward Will.

"Yes, of course, Bill," he said. "Or should I call you Mr. Stevenson? You know, I suggested that your dad have a lawyer look at it. It's right here."

Will slipped a folded piece of paper from his shirt pocket. "You'll see that everything's in order. No problems here." He looked at Charlotte. "Yes, your son will be done in a jiffy, so you might as well cut him that piece of pie. I mean, how could anyone say no to something so delicious?"

Chapter Nine

S am pulled his skateboard from the back of his car and watched Jordan do the same. His car was the only one parked in the high school parking lot, and he let out a sigh of relief. He was glad Paul and Jake weren't around. At least not yet.

It wasn't that Sam was embarrassed by his friends . . . well, at least that wasn't the biggest reason. He mostly just hated the tension in the air between him and Jordan and wanted that cleared up before more people were brought into the picture.

He felt bad though, knowing that Emily and Christopher would be waiting to see them, even though his grandma reaffirmed they'd have time over the week to spend with Jordan.

"So this is where you go to high school?" Jordan eyed the brick building with a puzzled look on his face.

Sam knew the school was as different from their high school in San Diego as it possibly could be. To Sam, Bedford High School looked like the school in the classic movie *Back to the Future*. In contrast, their high school in San Diego could be compared to an outdoor mall with tall,

93

picture windows and breezy walkways. Their lockers had been outside because the weather was always nice.

Sam watched Jordan's face, wondering if he was making the same comparisons between "cool" and "lame," but Jordan glanced away before Sam could guess his thoughts.

Jordan dropped his board, stepped on it, and pushed off with one foot, gliding across the asphalt parking lot, getting his bearings. The ride home hadn't been silent, but the excitement they had felt when Jordan first arrived hadn't returned either. Instead, they'd mostly talked about life in San Diego, people they both knew, and Jordan's plans for after graduation.

Sam, of course, had nothing exciting to share about Bedford. More than that, his plans for the future were about as solid as the clouds that drifted lazily overhead.

Sam wiped the sweat from his forehead and then moved to the sidewalk, where he planted his board near the curb. He thought about showing Jordan the new 360 he'd recently mastered, but even that didn't sound like fun.

Jordan did some tricks on the flat expanse of the parking lot, but he did them without a smile or the shouts and cheers that usually accompanied his skating.

Sam's stomach rumbled, and he remembered he hadn't eaten much of the fast food they'd stopped for earlier. He glanced at the sun that was starting its descent into the horizon and figured his grandma most likely had dinner in the oven. If they left soon they'd be able to join the family.

Still, something inside Sam made him hesitant to take Jordan home with him. He stood on his board and zipped down the sidewalk, turning his body to guide the skateboard smoothly around the corner.

If his friend had made fun of those guys at the restaurant what would he say about Uncle Pete? Or Grandpa? And what would he think about a country music singer coming to the farm?

The more Sam thought about it, the more the air around him seemed to grow heavy, pressing down upon his shoulders. He sucked in a big breath of hot, muggy air and wished he could just skate away.

Instead, Sam skated out to Jordan. "Hey, what do you think about picking up some pizza and taking it over to my friend Paul's house? We can play video games and hang out and stuff."

"Guys play video games around here?" Jordan asked.

Sam tried to pretend that comment didn't annoy him. "Yeah, but instead of car races we play games with tractor races. And instead of war games, we see who can be the first one to scatter seeds on a field. Yeah, those are our video games." Sam shook his head.

Jordan kicked up his board and then grabbed it with his hand. "Hey, you don't have to be sarcastic. I was just asking. I mean, I didn't think—"

"Yeah, maybe you didn't." Sam interrupted, striding back toward his car with his board in hand.

"Hey, wait. Is this how it's going to be the whole time? 'Cause if it is, you might as well drive me back to the airport, and I'll hang out there until my flight home."

Sam paused and turned. Jordan was still standing in the same spot in the middle of the parking lot. He had a dejected look on his face. It was the same look, in fact, that Jordan had had when they were eight and he'd accidentally broken Sam's favorite water pistol.

Sam let out a low sigh. "No. It doesn't have to be this way. Just as long as you . . . as you . . ." He paused, trying to figure out what to say. "As long as you keep your thoughts to yourself. Yeah, Nebraska is lame. Or at least parts of it are. But for the next year at least, I have to deal with it. So stop reminding me how different everything is. I'm stuck here, and, well . . ." Sam looked down and kicked at a rock with his scuffed shoe. "There are some things I actually like."

He turned back and wondered what Jordan thought of *that* confession. He got in and stuck his keys into the ignition. Ten seconds later Jordan tossed his board through the half-open side window into the backseat and also got in.

"Does your friend have Dark Journey 2?" Jordan asked.

"Yeah, actually it's Paul's favorite game."

"No one can beat me at that game." Jordan rolled down the window and rested his arm on the door.

"Wanna bet?" Sam asked, starting the engine and backing up. "Dude, prepare to be crushed."

As he glanced in the rearview mirror, he noticed the softest hint of a smile in his own reflection.

Chapter
Ten

Emily ran her fingers over the edges of the gilded frame she carried and glanced back at her grandma and Christopher, who also carried framed photographs. They'd already taken Christopher's Lego creations to the open-class section, and now it was Emily's turn to enter her photos at the arts and crafts building.

She'd been excited all day—eager to be here, doing this. She'd let her mind wander in church this morning, thinking about the photos she liked best. Then, when they picked up the enlargements from that nice photo guy, she'd thought about seeing them framed and hanging on the exhibit wall.

Even as she framed her prints, she'd tried to picture all the people who'd be looking at them. Yet, now that she was here, actually doing this, Emily wasn't so sure.

"Do you think these frames look okay?" she asked again. They'd found all three frames in the attic. They were as old as her grandpa, maybe older . . . and they looked it. She just wished she'd had money to buy new, fancy frames for her photos.

"I told you, it makes them look original. Lots of people pay big money for antique frames like these." Grandma sounded positive and upbeat, but Emily was skeptical. They just looked old to her.

The three of them walked back past the sign that read, WELCOME TO THE FAIR. There were other young people filtering in from the parking lot, all of them carrying items to enter in the arts and crafts division.

"Grandma, did you ever have anything go to the state level?" Emily asked, trying to get her mind off her worries about the competition.

"Yes, actually I did. When I was eleven or twelve, I was in 4-H and my mom gave me the idea of making a prairie skirt."

"What's that? Is it a skirt to pray in? Get it? Prayer-ee." Christopher laughed at his own joke.

"No, just a long skirt with flowered material and lace on the bottom," Grandma explained. "So I made the skirt and remember vividly having to redo the hem three times."

"And you won?" Emily felt her heartbeat quickening the closer she got to the exhibit building.

"Well, yes," Grandma continued, "we went to the county fair and there was my skirt with a blue ribbon on it. I was so excited. But the lady in charge of the sewing section said I was too young to go to the state fair."

"Did you cry?" Christopher asked.

"Yes, I believe I shed a few tears. I remember being disappointed and walking back to our 4-H booth. Then, a few minutes later, another one of the girls in my group ran up to me and said the judge wanted to talk to me. Turns out, they said I could enter my skirt at the state level after all."

"Did you go to Omaha?"

"Actually, we did. We only went for one day, but it's a day I'll never forget. Of course, the best thing was that blue ribbon got me excited about sewing," Charlotte continued, "and I've been doing it ever since."

"Did you win at the state level?" Christopher asked.

"No, unfortunately I didn't, but I still have that skirt and the blue ribbon around the attic somewhere. Maybe I'll find it one day."

"That's great, Grandma, really great." Emily bit her lip, seeing that the line to the arts and crafts building stretched out the front door of the exhibit hall. Many of the kids had wagons or boxes filled with projects, and they stood there with confidence and eagerness. Emily slowed her footsteps, regretting she'd come and wondering what Grandma would do if she turned around and said she wanted to return to the farm.

Christopher readjusted the frame in his hands.

"Don't drop it. Be careful," Emily scolded.

"I won't, I won't. I'm not a baby, Emily."

"Emily, Christopher, be nice. No arguing."

They neared the building, and Emily smiled at the girl and her mom standing in front of her. Then she turned back to her grandma.

"I can remember when they first built this building," Grandma was saying. "I was just a little girl."

"Uh-huh," Emily said, pretending she was listening to Grandma. Instead her gaze moved down the line of waiting young people, checking out the photographs they were entering and sizing up their entries against her own. One thing she noticed was that they all had nice, new frames.

"Looks like we got here just in time. They're only accepting entries for fifteen more minutes. We almost missed it."

"Grandma, look!" Christopher pointed to the horse barn two buildings down. Outside it a large trailer was parked and a teen boy was leading out a row of miniature horses.

"Can we go look, Grandma? Please?"

"Not today. Today is still a set-up day. But I promise, once the fair opens, the horse barn will be one of the first places we stop."

"Can we look at them when we bring back the flowers and vegetables to enter?" Christopher asked. "Toby might want to see them too. I bet she's never seen a horse the same size as her."

"We'll see," Grandma said. "And speaking of Toby, we need to sign you up for the showmanship category."

"Today? Seriously?" Christopher's eyes widened.

"Well, you don't perform today, but you sign up."

Emily pressed her framed photo to her chest. "Why don't you go ahead and sign Christopher up. I can carry all three frames." Emily hoped her voice sounded convincing.

Charlotte glanced at her watch. "Well, it is getting close to the cutoff. Are you sure you don't mind standing here alone?"

"No, Grandma. I'll be fine, honestly."

"All right then. Hang around this area when you're done, okay?"

Emily nodded, and then she watched as Grandma strode off with Christopher half-walking, half-skipping at her side.

As she stood there with the heavy frames in her hands, Emily tried to convince herself that everything would be okay. Just in front of her, another teen girl had a wagon with five framed prints stacked inside. The one on top was a beautiful photo of white, fluffy clouds hanging over a bright, red barn. The photo looked perfect, just like the girl. It looked professional. Worthy of a blue ribbon.

Emily tried to think of some excuse for leaving the line. Maybe she could tell her grandma she had to go the bathroom really bad. Or maybe she would say she saw someone she knew.

Emily stepped out of line and turned. Yet she'd only taken two steps when she heard someone loudly calling her name.

"Emily Slater, oh my goodness, are those your photos? Let me see them."

Emily turned to see Ashley's face smiling at her. "Uh, Ashley. Hi."

"Where are you going? I think they're going to close registration soon. Then they won't accept any more entries."

Emily didn't know what to say. She bit her lip and forced a smile.

"Wait a minute. Were you trying to sneak out without entering them?" Ashley shook her head, and her red hair danced around her face. "Please don't tell me you were leaving."

"Well, this is my first year, and I don't want to look stupid. My photos are not as good as the others I've seen."

"Now, why in the world do you think you'd look stupid?" Ashley held out her hands. "Let me see those photographs."

"No, not here."

"Yes, here." The set of Ashley's chin made her look like her mother, and Emily didn't dare argue.

Ashley took the first photograph and then held it out in front of her as if she were hanging it on an invisible wall.

"No way. You took these photos? That baby goat is *so* cute!"

A few people looked over their shoulders, taking in the scene, and Emily felt heat rising to her cheeks.

"And I love this one of the sunflower. Oh, and look at the one of the steer and dog. I love them! What don't you like about them?"

Emily leaned close to Ashley. "The frames. They're totally old and stupid."

"The frames? What's wrong with the frames?"

Suddenly Hannah Carter's voice broke in, and Emily turned to see her grandma's friend standing behind her.

Oh great, just what I need. As soon as Emily saw Mrs. Carter, she knew she was facing a losing battle. Ashley was persuasive enough, but with Mrs. Carter there too . . . Well, Emily took a step closer to the line.

"I saw you girls, and it looks like you have something fun to enter," Mrs. Carter commented, looking at the photos and glancing from face to face, trying to figure out who they belonged to.

"Yes, I was going to enter these photos," Emily confessed. "But, well, I thought I'd just wait until next year. You know, when I know more about how this whole thing works."

"Yes, I came right in time. I saw Emily trying to slip out of line, and I ruined her plans of escape." Ashley smiled and held up the framed photograph for Mrs. Carter to see. "I mean, why wouldn't someone enter a photograph as cool as this?"

"Just you wait a minute." Mrs. Carter tilted Emily's face up toward hers with her free hand. "You're not worried about competing, are you?"

Emily nodded. Still, she knew Grandma's friend well enough to know what was to come.

"Why, that reminds me of the time on *The Brady Bunch* when Marcia was running for class president. It was Marcia, wasn't it?" She released Emily's face and stroked her own chin.

"Okay, okay. You don't need to tell me the episode." Emily stepped back into line, ignoring the looks of the kids in front of her.

Mrs. Carter winked. "That's my girl. Good decision, because you know me. I wouldn't let you *not* enter."

"Yes, Mrs. Carter. I know you." Emily grinned. "And you can go tell Grandma that you found me and encouraged me. She doesn't have to worry. In fact, both of you can tell her that."

Mrs. Carter's jaw dropped, and a spurt of laughter burst from Ashley.

Emily winked. "I figured it out, didn't I?"

Mrs. Carter laughed. "Okay, girl, I'll go tell her." She nudged Ashley with her elbow. "So we were caught, weren't we?"

"Yeah, your grandma was the one who put us up to coming over here," Ashley confessed. "But I'm telling the truth. Those are amazing pictures."

"Thanks." Emily eyed the one with the sunflower again, admitting she did like it, despite the frame.

"Well, I'd better get back to work. We're setting up the pie booth, and I'm painting a new sign." Mrs. Carter swept her hand across the air. "How do you like the name *Amen Pies*?"

"Amen Pies?" Emily wrinkled her nose.

"Yes, and underneath the name in bold letters it says, 'Pies so good you'll shout *Amen* after every bite.'"

Ashley chuckled. "I love it."

Emily nodded, thinking it wasn't something that would fly in San Diego, but it worked in Bedford. "I agree."

"Good thing you do, because the sign's almost done." Mrs. Carter gave Emily a quick hug. "See you later."

"See you later," Emily called, and in a strange way she felt better about her entries, even if Grandma had sent Mrs. Carter and Ashley over to encourage her. At least they cared. At least they liked the photos.

"Amen after every bite," Emily mumbled to herself.

"Only Hannah Carter would come up with something like that," Ashley added. "I have to run too. I promised my mom I'd take lunch orders and get right back. This is the only week of the year we're open on Sunday. I'm going to have a riot from the fair office people coming in if I don't get hustling."

Ashley hurried off with a wave, and before Emily knew it, it was her turn to enter her photographs.

The woman at the registration tables checked the forms, taped them onto the frames, and then glanced up to Emily with a wide smile. "We've got everything we need, sweetheart. Good luck."

"Thanks." Emily walked out of the arts and crafts exhibit hall and to her surprise found Grandma and Christopher waiting outside. As she approached them, she let out a long sigh.

"Okay, all done."

It *was* done, Emily realized. Her photos were entered, and that was that. Whether she won or not, she guessed it didn't matter much. As Grandma, Ashley, and Mrs. Carter had reminded her, trying was good enough.

Besides, she had other things to think about now, like maybe getting photographs of the video shoot. She couldn't wait until the whole crew showed up, and she wondered what Jordan would say about that. It wasn't like everyone had a music video shot in their backyard.

Emily rubbed her hands together at the thought. "Yeah, that will be fun."

SUNDAY MORNING Sam glanced at his cell phone, surprised that he hadn't received a phone call from his grandma, to ask if he and Jordan would be meeting the family at church. He was sure to hear about that later.

Jordan, Paul, and Jake were still slumbering in sleeping bags on the living room floor where they'd finally crashed after playing video games most of the night.

Last night after pizza, they'd just started playing video games when Grandma had called to check on them. Reluctantly, she'd agreed that they could spend the night at Paul's house.

As Sam rose and stretched, his grandma's words replayed in his mind. "I guess one night will be fine if we have your friend here for the rest of the week." Although she had sounded fine, Sam felt bad about it. It wasn't like he didn't appreciate all his grandparents had done for him and his brother and sister. It was just that his grandparents were different from people in San Diego. Different from Jordan's family and everyone else Jordan knew.

Someone knocked on a door elsewhere in the house, interrupting Sam's thoughts. He guessed the sound was coming from the direction of the kitchen. Sam could hear Paul's mom answering it. Then he heard girls' voices, and he nudged Paul's side with his foot. "Get up. It looks like we have company."

The voices grew louder, and Sam combed his fingers through his hair, trying to make it lie flat. Realizing it still stuck up in every direction, he looked around for his baseball cap. Finally he found it under his pillow and slipped it on.

The girls laughed at something going on in the kitchen, and as if finally understanding what was going on, Jake, Paul, and Jordan sat up, nearly in unison, kicking off the sleeping bags. None of them had bothered to change last night, and all still wore the shorts and T-shirts they'd worn the previous day.

Sam slumped down on the couch. He wiped the sleep from his eyes and tried to pretend he'd been awake for a while.

Paul's mom entered the room and opened the drapes. "Rise and shine, boys. The day's half over, and you have company."

Arielle and her friend Jessica entered the room. Jessica liked either Jake or Paul—Sam just wasn't sure which one yet. And with them was another girl Sam didn't recognize.

"Hey there," Arielle glanced in Sam's direction and held back a grin. "I called your house, and your grandma said you were here. We thought we'd stop by. I wanted you to meet my cousin Natalie. She's here from Kansas."

Sam vaguely remembered Arielle telling him a cousin was coming, but he'd forgotten about it until now.

Natalie was slightly shorter than Arielle, and in Sam's opinion not as cute. But she seemed nice enough, and Sam couldn't help noticing her locking eyes with Jordan and offering him a warm smile.

"What are you guys doing today? If you don't have plans, I thought we could head down to Heather Creek for a swim."

"Wow, swimming. That sounds cool." Jordan stood and slipped his hands in his pockets. "I don't know about these bums, but you can count me in."

"Sure." Sam patted the couch beside him, and Arielle came over and sat by him. He felt like putting his arm around her—just to remind Jordan which of the girls was already taken, but he knew he hadn't showered yet or brushed his teeth, and he didn't want to get too close.

"Do you think your grandparents would mind, you know, if we all came out?"

Sam paused for a minute, wondering if he should call them, but then quickly changed his mind. His grandparents liked Arielle, and they were eager to meet Jordan.

"Nah, it will be fine. I bet we can even find Grandma cooking up something for lunch. She always makes a big meal after church."

"Cool. Jessica has her car, and we'll follow you guys out there." Arielle stood and walked toward the kitchen, looking at them expectantly.

"What? Right now?" Jake sat up and scratched his head. "I need to shower first."

"Shower to go swimming?" Natalie laughed and cast the same warm smile toward Jake she'd previously offered to Jordan.

"Yeah, we don't want to waste the day waiting for you guys. Get up, and let's get going. We'll meet you outside."

They walked back through the kitchen and out the door, and Sam glanced at the other guys.

"One thing's for sure. Nebraska girls are just as bossy as the ones in California." Jordan grabbed his sleeping bag and began to roll it up.

"And just as cute too," he mumbled only loud enough for Sam to hear. Then he glanced over, and Sam saw a glimmer in his friend's eye.

At least he likes something about Nebraska.

Chapter
Eleven

When they got back to the farm, no one was around so they all changed and headed down to the creek. Sam didn't realize Jordan hadn't followed the rest of them into the water until he turned and found his friend still standing on the shore.

Jordan's focus was on the muddy banks and the tall reeds that lined the shore. He lifted one foot and mud stuck to it. Then he wrinkled his nose and glanced out at Sam.

"Come on!" Sam yelled, splashing water in Jordan's direction. Next to Sam, Arielle treaded water, and he had to admit she looked cute with her hair wet and slicked back.

"Yeah, what are you waiting for, Mr. California?" Natalie, Arielle's cousin, called with a hint of flirting in her voice.

"You're kidding, right? How am I supposed to get out there?" Jordan pushed a cattail reed to the side.

"Those cattails aren't made of iron. Just move through them. It's not deep. See? I'm standing." Sam stood on his toes to make himself appear taller.

"I'm not worried about how deep it is. It's just . . . this mud is gross."

"Ah, come on. What are you, a sissy?" Paul dunked underwater and came up with a handful of mud. Before Sam realized what was happening, a ball of mud flew through the air and hit Jordan on the chest, sliding down the front of him.

"Jerk. Knock it off. That's gross!" Jordan wiped the mud off the best he could.

"Come on, Jordan. We used to go swimming all the time. Remember those swim lessons when we were five?" Sam tried to keep his tone light, but he had to agree with Paul; Jordan was being a sissy.

"That's different. We swam in pools . . . not in mud. This is totally disgusting." He knelt down and attempted to scoop up creek water to wipe the rest of the mud off his chest. "And this water. You can't even see through it."

"See through it?" Natalie asked.

"Yeah, to the bottom."

"Are you kidding? You don't want to see the bottom. Then you'd be able to see the fish . . . and the leeches." Jake laughed.

"Shut up!" Sam cupped his hand and splashed a huge wave of river water in Jake's face. "You're not helping."

"Hey, lighten up. Come on. You have to admit your friend is being a jerk. It's just a creek. And he's making a big deal out of it."

Sam looked from Paul and Jake to Jordan, and then back again.

"It's just a creek." Arielle touched Sam's arm. "We swim in it all the time. He either needs to get used to it, or he's going to have a totally miserable day."

Sam nodded. Then he waded closer to Jordan. "Just think of it as the ocean. We used to swim in the ocean too. And there are fish in there."

"But not leeches. I've never heard of ocean leeches." Jordan moved back up the shore, out of the mud, and opened up one of the towels, spreading it on the weeds.

"Seriously, just run and jump in. The water feels good." Sam pushed his way through the reeds near the shore and attempted to get his footing on the bank. His foot slipped, and he felt himself sliding forward. He tried to stop his fall with his hands but both of them sank into the mud to his wrists. He could hear laughter behind him, and Sam was sure he looked great with his rear sticking up in the air. He scrambled up the shore the best he could and then plopped down next to Jordan, trying to ignore his muddy hands and feet.

"We can walk up the bank a little. There's a rope swing. It's pretty fun."

"No thanks. Go ahead."

Sam felt the sun beating down on him. More than anything he wanted to say that Jordan could throw a hissy fit, but he wasn't going to put up with it. No one was going to put up with it. More than anything, Sam wanted to tell Jordan to sit there in the sun and bake if he wanted to, but Sam was going to swim with the others.

Yet when Sam opened his mouth, something inside told him that wouldn't be smart. Jordan, after all, was his best friend. Or at least he used to be.

More than that, Sam remembered what he had been like when he first came to Nebraska. He'd thought everything was stupid and disgusting too. The fact was, it had taken him a long time to adjust. Jordan had been here only two days.

Sam took a deep breath, knowing what his grandparents would tell him. He needed to be patient.

Sam sat there a while, plucking the blades of green grass that poked through the yellowish-brown weeds. He thought about what he could say and what he could do to make both his new friends and his old friend happy. Honestly, he couldn't think of a way to do it. Someone was going to be upset no matter what.

Side by side, he and Jordan watched the others laughing and splashing in the creek. Finally, Sam cleared his throat.

"You know, I think Natalie likes you."

"No sir." Jordan shook his head, but Sam was certain he saw Jordan's eyes widen in interest.

"Yeah, I think so. Look, see how she keeps looking up here?"

"Yeah, well, she is sort of cute."

"Yeah, not as pretty as Arielle, but not too bad."

"You're right, Arielle is pretty."

Sam's eyes darted to Jordan, and Jordan laughed. "Dude, don't flip out; I'm only joking. I'd never steal your girl."

"Not that you could if you tried."

"Yeah, you're right. Not that it would really work. It seems Arielle is into hicks and hick music. I mean, it's a good thing you told me that country-western CD was hers in your car, or I would have totally thought you'd gone off the deep end."

"It's hers. I don't listen to that stuff. I might adjust to

other things around here, but I'll never give up my rock."

They sat for a while longer, watching the others as they timed themselves to see how long they could hold their breath under water. Finally, when Sam thought he was going to pass out from heatstroke, Jordan stood up.

"So you say the rope swing is fun?"

"Yeah." Sam stood too. "It's fun." He nodded his chin upstream. "Wanna go try?"

"I bet I can do a flip off of it."

"Can not."

"Yeah, bet I can."

"Ten bucks says you're going to land flat on your back or do a belly flop." Sam stretched out his hand that was now caked with dry mud.

"I'll bet you, but I'm not going to shake." Then Jordan turned and headed up the river bank.

"Want to go to the rope swing?" Sam called to the others.

"Yeah!"

"Fun."

"Cool," the voices called. Then the others waded to shore.

Sam reached out a hand and helped Arielle onto the bank. Then he handed her a towel.

"Thanks for that, Sam." She wrapped the towel around her and then turned and helped Natalie up the bank.

"You're welcome. I think the towel is nice and warm from the sun."

"Yeah," she laughed. "Thanks for the towel too, but that wasn't what I was talking about. Thanks for sticking up for Jordan. I felt bad for him."

Sam shrugged. "He's my friend."

"You're a good friend. And a good boyfriend." Arielle took Sam's dirty hand and squeezed. Then she released it. "Race you to the swing."

Sam laughed and darted after her. He'd never understand girls, what they were thinking, or what they appreciated. But at least this time he'd done the right thing, according to Arielle. And, well, according to himself. Because as he raced up the shore after the others he felt good inside. Like things would work out. Like this week wouldn't be a total bomb after all.

WARM AIR AND SWEET SCENTS greeted Charlotte as she carried a basket of fresh vegetables into the kitchen. Picked fresh from the garden, the variety of vegetables would make a nice salad to welcome Jordan to the farm. As she scanned her kitchen counter she wondered if she'd gone overboard with dinner. The homemade biscuits were made. She'd sliced fresh onions to sauté with the pork chops. And from the oven came the yummy fragrance of peach cobbler. A salad and some fresh applesauce would finish the meal.

Sam and Jordan had arrived back from the creek and stayed only long enough to say a quick hello, before they headed upstairs for a shower. Charlotte now heard them listening to their rock music in Sam's room.

As she sliced tomatoes for the salad, she wondered how this visit would go. But as the stove's timer beeped, telling her the cobbler was done, she shook any worries out of her mind and looked forward to getting to know Jordan.

After the biscuits were baked and the gravy was simmering on the stove, Charlotte's stomach rumbled, and she knew dinnertime had come.

"Christopher," Charlotte said to her grandson, who was lying in front of the television watching a documentary on space travel, "can you please call everyone for dinner?"

Christopher stood and walked to the bottom of the stairs. "Dinner's ready!" he called.

Then he walked to the kitchen door, opening it and leaning outside. "Dinner's ready! Grandpa, Uncle Pete! Time for dinner."

Charlotte shook her head and chuckled. "Thank you, but I think I could have done that. Can you make sure—" The sentence wasn't even out of her mouth when Charlotte heard the pounding of footsteps coming down the stairs. Sam, Jordan, and Emily entered in mid-conversation that had something to do with the best burgers in San Diego.

Ten seconds later the kitchen door opened, and Bob, Pete, and Dana entered.

Christopher looked at Charlotte with a smirk, and she smiled back. "Boy, you sure have a good set of lungs. Who needs a bullhorn with you around?"

"Huh?" Christopher scratched his head.

"Want me to put this on the table for you?" Dana grabbed the basket that held the fresh biscuits wrapped in a dish towel.

"Grandma, can I put the lemonade on the table too?" Emily asked. "Oh, and the yummy salad." She grabbed the pitcher of lemonade and the big bowl of salad and set them near her place at the table.

"We pretty much have salad every day. You're acting like it's a new thing." Sam smirked, elbowing Jordan. "You're lucky you don't have a sister."

Jordan chuckled. "Yeah. I guarantee my brother wouldn't be excited about salad for dinner. I mean . . ." Jordan glanced sheepishly at Charlotte. "Uh, not that anything's wrong with salad, Mrs. Stevenson. This one looks great. It's just that my brother doesn't really like vegetables."

Charlotte pointed to the chair next to where Sam usually sat, motioning for Jordan to have a seat. "Oh, I understand. No worries. I have to say that, growing up, Pete didn't care for vegetables either."

"Yeah, not until Dad told me I needed to eat them to grow up big and strong," Pete joined in. "So I did. After all, it became my main goal in life to grow taller than Denise."

The room quieted, and Charlotte didn't know if it was because Bob was already folding his hands, or because of the mention of her daughter's name.

"Shall we pray?" Bob said, breaking the silence.

Charlotte folded her hands, wondering if Jordan was used to such rituals at home. He didn't seem bothered by it, and he removed his baseball cap and placed it on his lap before bowing his head.

"Gracious Father, we thank Thee for your provisions today," Bob prayed. "We thank Thee that Jordan arrived safely and that we can look forward to the week ahead in which we will celebrate the bounty of the land. In your Son, Jesus's name, amen."

"Amen," the voices around the table said in unison. As Sam poured lemonade into his glass and Jordan's, Jordan took a large pork chop from the serving platter for himself and placed another on Sam's plate.

Charlotte was pleased to see that Jordan wasn't shy about serving himself or filling his plate with food. She also liked to see the way the guys seemed natural around each other.

"So did you have a nice flight?" Charlotte asked Jordan as she scooped salad onto her plate.

"Oh, yes ma'am. I thought I would fall asleep right away, but I started reading this book, and it turned out to be pretty good."

"Do you like to read, Jordan?" Dana's face brightened.

Jordan shrugged and glanced around the table. "Sometimes, I suppose."

Sam chuckled, and Jordan elbowed him in the ribs. Sitting side by side, Charlotte noticed how much taller Jordan was than Sam. And thinner too. But with Jordan's boyish face and round blue eyes, he seemed younger. He didn't have that tough edge that Sam always tried to affect.

"Tell my grandparents about the time my mom took us to the library and we got kicked out," Sam mumbled with his mouth full of food.

"Kicked out? Really?" Pete eyed Jordan as if he suddenly had a new respect for the young man.

Jordan shrugged. "Yeah, well, we thought the tiny elevator that carried books between floors was really cool. But I guess we gave the upstairs librarian quite a scare when she opened the door and saw two boys sitting there."

"All we said was boo." Sam smirked.

Laughter erupted around the table, and Charlotte tried to picture Denise's reaction.

Sam took a drink of lemonade. "Yeah, my mom insisted that we volunteer there every Saturday for a month. Although I think she thought it was a better idea than the head librarian did."

Jordan laughed as another memory was resurrected, and Charlotte was almost afraid to ask.

Sam glanced at Jordan and must have understood what his friend was thinking, because he quickly changed the topic. "Hey, Grandma, I was wondering. Do you have a calendar or something for the fair? I want to take Jordan to the demolition derby."

"There are other things you don't want to miss—like the dog show," Christopher butted in.

"Or the art display." Emily grinned.

"Exactly." Jordan nodded.

"Yes, the fair-events calendar is over there under the pile of mail." Charlotte pointed to the counter. "There's always more to do than time to do it, but I'm glad Jordan decided to come for fair week. It's always full of excitement, unlike ordinary summer days."

"Unless you call chores exciting," Sam mumbled.

"Fair week kicks off with the parade on Tuesday, followed by the opening of the fairgrounds and all the rides." Charlotte tucked her hair behind her ear. "Although, truth be told, I'm not sure that we'll be able to attend all the fair activities, especially with all the excitement happening around the farm."

"It's so crazy." Pete shook his head. "I knew of one, maybe two, of that woman's songs. And now that she's coming to

Bedford and filming that silly video on the farm, I hear her everywhere. On the radio. In television commercials."

"Yeah, I even saw her photo on the cover of *Teen* magazine," Dana said. "She's super cute." She chuckled. "It's not fair, really, to have those looks *and* that voice."

Pete wiped biscuit crumbs off his lips and then glanced over at Dana. "She's not as pretty as you."

Pink rose to Dana's cheeks, and Charlotte could tell she was pleased by the comment.

"I have to admit I feel the same way, Pete. Shae Lynne was even on *Good Morning—*"

"Shae Lynne?" Jordan interrupted, his light blue eyes widening. "Did your grandma just say Shae Lynne?" He turned in his chair, grabbed Sam's shoulders, and shook them. "Is that the video Emily was talking about on the phone earlier? A video for a country music star?"

Sam grimaced.

"Sam didn't tell you yet?" Charlotte cocked an eyebrow at Sam.

Jordan's eyes widened. "No, Sam said they were filming a milk commercial, starring Trudy the cow."

Sam smiled and flipped his long bangs out of his eyes. "No, I didn't tell you it was a milk commercial. I said they were shooting a video and Trudy was going to be in it. You just assumed it was a milk commercial and that our cow was the star."

"So what kind of video is it? Is Shae Lynne going to be singing?" Jordan started to pick up his fork but then put it down again, too distracted to eat. He folded his arms over his chest.

"Oh yes. It's a music video for one of Shae Lynne's new

songs." Charlotte hoped her feigned excitement made up for all of them.

"A music video? She's going to be singing?" Jordan asked. Then, remembering that he was a guest, he bit his bottom lip. "No offense. I just would rather listen to rock. I'm sure she's a nice, uh, person."

"Speaking of nice people," Charlotte cut in, "did Will call about what time everyone is coming?" She poured a tall glass of lemonade for herself.

"Yes, well, I was going to talk to you about that." Bob rubbed his chin as if trying to remember the conversation. "The whole crew will be here around one o'clock tomorrow."

"One o'clock tomorrow?" The list of all she had to do tomorrow scrolled through Charlotte's mind.

"So, I suppose it's a go?" She used her fork to move around the food on her plate.

"Well, Bill read through the contract and said that it looked in order, but he took the extra copy with him to read it in more detail. He's supposed to call us back before bedtime. But as far as I can figure, unless Bill sees a major problem, it's going to happen."

"So the video people are *really* going to be here tomorrow?" Emily placed a hand over her heart.

Jordan poked Emily's shoulder. "*You* should have at least told me. You're *never* able to keep secrets."

"Ha-ha, very funny. I *can* keep a secret. Besides, Christopher and I were going to tell you, but Sam wanted us to wait. He thought you would just make fun of it."

"Maybe we can just stay in town with Paul and Jake and steer clear of the whole thing." Sam took another biscuit from the basket and slathered it with butter.

"Seriously?" Emily cocked an eyebrow. "You can't dislike country music that bad."

"Wanna make a bet?"

"I'll bet you about that, or about anything!" Christopher jumped in, excited that the conversation had finally come around to something worth talking about.

"You really want to bet, buddy?" Jordan eyed Christopher from around the table. "I bet I can make a rock skip more times across the creek than you can."

Christopher's shoulders sank. "I don't know how to skip."

"Really, it's easy. I'll show you."

"After dinner?" Christopher perked up.

Then Jordan turned to Charlotte. "If that's okay with you, ma'am."

"Yes, of course, Jordan."

As Charlotte finished her meal, she let out a small sigh of contentment. For the previous week she'd thought about all the work that needed to get done—including caring for a guest. But what she hadn't remembered was that even in the midst of busy days and weeks, God sometimes opens up a window of grace too. And this was one of those moments, when they could just enjoy being together.

In fact, moments like this were what made life at Heather Creek Farm different from most places. Yes, they were busy. But at least they were busy together.

Chapter
Twelve

For as long as Charlotte could remember, Monday morning of fair week meant getting up before dawn, doing morning chores, and loading up all the fresh flowers, vegetables, and baked goods she'd planned on entering in the fair. Followed, of course, by a fair board meeting in which all the final kinks got worked out of the well-oiled fair machine.

Things had gone well during Jordan's first night on the farm. She'd been disappointed that the boys had missed church, but she decided it was a battle for another day. After dinner the kids skipped rocks down at the creek, and then Sam had given Jordan a quick tour of the farm, and they'd watched a movie with Emily.

Charlotte had been surprised, but pleased, when Bill called to say the contract was on the up-and-up. She knew if anyone could find a legal reason not to sign the contract it would have been Bill. And as for having more people on the farm, making more demands, Charlotte didn't know how it could be much different than how things already were. Her life wasn't her own, and hadn't been for quite a while.

But enough of that, she thought. *I'll worry about the video shoot when the time comes. Now I just need to concentrate on the fair.* She glanced around and again took in the sight of the busy fairgrounds, breathing in the scents.

Charlotte's stomach growled at the aroma of mini-donuts and funnel cakes, and she realized she hadn't eaten breakfast. Even though she hated the thought of paying so much for a small container of donuts, the smell drew her in. *Later,* she told her stomach. *I promise.*

Beside her, Christopher pulled a wagon filled with her entries. Although he'd yawned in the car during the ride to town, now his eyes were wide as he took in the temporary city that had been built within the chain-link fencing. A giggle spilled from his lips as they passed the hog barn and a dozen squeals—high-pitched and sharp—split the air.

Charlotte tried to see the world through the eyes of someone who hadn't grown up with this yearly tradition. She took in the clear blue sky, the white benches, and the green buildings shaded by large trees. And beyond the exhibition area the rides were still being set up. How many loops had she taken around the Ferris wheel during her lifetime? Too many to count.

A security guard drove by in a golf cart, and two fair volunteers walked by sporting matching yellow aprons. Charlotte had forgotten her own apron, folded and on top of the dryer, but she knew she'd pick it up the next time she went home.

This morning as she was lying in bed, Charlotte had almost talked herself out of entering the sunflowers, the wildflower bouquet, and the fresh vegetables from her garden as she had planned. Yet as the minutes ticked by, she knew she didn't have that choice. After all, she was the one who'd talked the kids into entering items. What type of example would she be to Emily and Christopher if she slacked off this year?

Come on. Get in the spirit. The fair only comes once a year. Enjoy it, she'd told herself.

And now she was enjoying it. Bits and pieces of joy seemed to come upon her at the most unexpected moments during her hectic days. Yet inside, something felt different, and Charlotte finally came to the realization that she was grieving for the way fair days had been for her until recently.

Instead of shuttling kids around, she'd been able to spend time with her friends. She'd strolled around the fair with Bob. She'd relaxed and just enjoyed seeing everyone in her community in one place. She'd enjoyed the fair in ways that weren't possible for her now.

The wagon wheels squeaked beside her, and Charlotte reminded herself of the things she still *would* be able to enjoy about this week: the fair queen with the big crown; the 4-H members with their white, pressed dress shirts; seventy-pound girls leading around fifteen-hundred-pound steers; the exhibits and the projects her neighbors had been working on for months.

"Hey, Grandma, you're walking too fast," Christopher called, and Charlotte slowed her steps.

"Testing, one, two, three," a man's voice said over the loudspeaker, checking the announcement system. Charlotte recognized it as Bob's voice, and that alone made her smile.

Just like yesterday when Emily brought in her photographs, lines of people again waited outside the buildings to submit their entries in other categories. Some people, she knew, entered more than two hundred items in the various events. Years ago, Charlotte had tried to match that pace, but not anymore. She entered what she managed to get together, and the rest . . . Well, she could try again next year.

Charlotte waved to friends she knew and watched as dutiful husbands ran around with wagons similar to the one Christopher pulled, helping their wives get everything ready to submit.

"Every year I get sucked into this," one man complained to another as they walked by. Charlotte couldn't help but chuckle under her breath, inwardly feeling their pain.

CHARLOTTE TOOK A SIP of burned coffee and watched as the other fair board members filtered into the meeting room. Her items were entered, and now Christopher was content walking the animal barns until her meeting finished.

She smiled at Ned and Betty as they entered and noticed that her smile wasn't returned. Instead, as soon as the meeting was called to order, eyes turned to her.

"Is Bob coming?" Dwayne asked.

"No, he's busy this morning working at the arena. I heard him testing out the announcement system not too long ago."

She noticed whispers among the other board members but couldn't make out their comments. Her stomach tightened into a big ball of tension. "Is there a problem?"

Dwayne folded his hands on the table in front of him. "Well, I wouldn't say it's a problem, but more of a concern. Word has gotten around town that Heather Creek Farm is going to be featured in a music video."

"Yes, we were fortunate to be offered the opportunity." Charlotte didn't know what else to say. After all, she'd questioned whether or not they should accept the offer.

Charlotte heard footsteps behind her, and she turned to see Hannah entering. Charlotte let out a sigh of relief, seeing her friend's face. Hannah offered a soft smile.

"Are you all jealous?" Hannah jutted out her chin. "Is that what this is about?" She sat on the metal chair with a flourish.

"Well, the Stevensons' farm did just win Adams County Farm of the Year. Is it fair that they get chosen for this too?"

"It's not that we went looking for it." Charlotte heard her voice rise an octave, and more than anything she wished Bob were here.

"Jealousy is not the point," Dwayne injected. "It's just that the fair has put out a lot of money to bring Shae Lynne into the area."

"Yup, a lot of money. More than we've ever spent before," Ned echoed.

"And?" Charlotte glanced around at the faces around the table. A few of the board members looked her in the eye, but most of them focused on everything but her—the walls, the ceiling, a piece of Scotch tape stuck to the table.

"We just think that maybe since we paid so much to bring Shae Lynne in some of that money they're paying for the use of your farm should come back to the fair," Ned's wife Betty commented.

Charlotte felt the hairs on the back of her neck stand up.

She didn't know what to say, or even what the right answer was. So she just sat there, in silence, wishing she was anywhere else.

"Now, don't think we don't understand you probably need that money to help with your grandkids, but I've heard people talking, Charlotte," Dwayne continued. "All around town everyone is going on and on about the music video. It's fair week, and they're not even talking about the fair."

"What if attendance drops?" Ned stuck out his chest, as if making his point stronger. "I mean, what if instead of attending the fair people head out to your farm to watch the making of that video?"

"Now, that won't happen." Charlotte felt her hands tremble. "We're not going to let anyone on the farm. What do you think? We're going to be selling tickets or something?"

She took a deep breath. "Here you go again. Do you hear yourselves?" She scanned the faces around the table. "This is exactly the flip side to what we were just talking about a few days ago. First, we were wondering about how to spend all the money we're going to make. And now we're worried about not making any money at all. Don't you think . . ." Charlotte felt her emotions building, and she tried to swallow them down. "Don't you think that we should wait and see how the week goes?"

Charlotte considered mentioning that she and Bob saw this extra money as an answer to their prayers. Or mentioning that she'd rather not have the video people there either. Or commenting on how excited the kids were at this opportunity. Instead, she just sat there, questioning where the fun in fair week had gone.

They continued on with their meeting, and thankfully

no one brought up the video or the money again. Instead, they talked about the rodeo, fair security, and a hundred other minor details Charlotte was no longer concerned about.

Thirty minutes later, the meeting was over, and Charlotte attempted to slip out of the office as quietly as possible. She'd barely gotten outside the door when she felt an arm slipping into hers. She knew without turning that it was Hannah.

"Hey, you okay?" Hannah rested her head on Charlotte's shoulder.

Charlotte shrugged. "Yeah, I suppose."

"You need to remember, Charlotte, that they're just volunteers. They're not professionals doing this, you know. They haven't been trained in human relations, and this is the first time anything like this has come up."

"Yes, well, it's not like this happens every day to us, either," Charlotte said, trying to keep her voice even, telling herself that Hannah was only trying to help. Reminding herself that the fair would go on, this week would pass, and the country music star would drive off into the sunset.

"You going to talk to Bob about it?"

Charlotte shrugged. "I don't know. I'm not sure. I really don't want to upset him."

"You should say something, Charlotte. Bob has broad shoulders. You need to remember that he can take a lot. More than you'd think sometimes."

"You're right." Charlotte offered a soft smile. Yet inside she questioned why all of this was happening. *Why this? Why now? Why us?*

The questions were there, but no answers came. Instead, Charlotte just listened as Hannah went on about the latest news concerning their neighbors.

As Charlotte listened, she realized that while Hannah was talking about the latest news concerning others, people around the fair were most likely talking about her and her family, yet again.

Oh, the joys of living in Bedford, where everybody's business is your business.

And vice versa.

Chapter
Thirteen

Charlotte was thankful to see Pete's truck sitting in the driveway when she arrived back at Heather Creek Farm. Yet she could hardly see Lazarus because of the large vehicles surrounding it. On either side of Pete's truck and behind it, long trucks were parked. Men and women scurried around unloading props and equipment.

Charlotte parked in the gravel just beyond the driveway and climbed out of her car. Christopher jumped out too, pausing in the driveway with wide eyes.

"Whoa," he said. "It's like Hollywood landed on our front lawn."

"Whoa is right." Charlotte swallowed down a lump in her throat.

Up ahead, Pete was talking to a group of people on the porch. Charlotte quickened her footsteps. Christopher tagged along behind her.

"Who needs the fair when we have this?" Christopher squealed.

Yeah, who needs the fair? Charlotte thought. Mostly because her heart still felt a little hurt from the comments of the other fair board members. Then again, weighing

against that hurt, she also couldn't wait for the fair to officially begin and to feel the energy of the fairgrounds and see
all the smiles. She couldn't wait to walk through the exhibition halls and to peek inside the food building and check
for ribbons on her pies. She'd won best of show six times,
and she wondered if this year would make seven.

She tried to forget the comments from the other fair
board members and instead decided to focus on welcoming
the group of strangers to their farm.

She approached the porch steps and waved to Will,
Buck, and two women who were standing with them. Both
women wore pointy-toed high-heeled shoes, and Charlotte
couldn't help but wonder how long those shoes would last
in the muck and dirt of the farm.

Will stretched out his hand and offered a big smile.
"Charlotte, I'd like you to meet Tami and Tracy. They are
Shae Lynne's assistants, and you'll be seeing them around
a lot."

"Nice to meet you both." Charlotte asked about their
trip and what they thought about Bedford. They answered
her questions but didn't warm to her, even when she
offered them each a glass of lemonade. They all declined.

From the corner of her eye Charlotte saw four men
easing a large camera down a ramp, coming closer to her
vegetable garden than she would have liked. Just as she was
about to mention something about them squishing her
tomatoes, she spotted Sam, Emily, and Jordan emerging
from the barn. Charlotte didn't want to be overbearing—or
to act like a meddling old woman—so instead of worrying
about the garden she asked the next question on her mind.

"Is Shae Lynne here?" Charlotte glanced around.

"No, sorry," Tami answered curtly. "Shae Lynne will be arriving in town tomorrow or the next day. The film crew will do some scenery shots over the next couple of days, and she'll most likely be joining us later in the week."

Tami seemed bored by the conversation. She was petite and dark-haired with a pixie face that would be rather pretty if she smiled. But she didn't smile. Not even close.

"Well, we'll be eager to meet her when the time comes. It's not a rock video, but I think the kids will be talking about this for a long time," Charlotte explained.

"Yes, of course. It's an event *many* people would be honored to be a part of." Tami glanced at the approaching teens and then turned back to Charlotte. "I'm sure Shae Lynne would personally like to thank your family for inviting us to your home."

The other assistant Tracy, who had blonde hair and large green eyes, smiled softly.

As Sam, Jordan, and Emily came closer, their words drifted ahead of them.

"Too bad this wasn't a rock video." Sam scanned the cameras.

"Dude, did you see that? They have a whole wardrobe thing filled with cowboy boots and cowboy hats. John Wayne would be jealous." Jordan laughed.

"I can't believe Shae Lynne's really going to be here," Emily commented, ignoring the guys.

A man walked by carrying a rhinestone jacket and chaps on a hanger, protected inside a clear plastic bag.

"Man, this is totally entertaining." Jordan remarked as

he slapped his leg and plunked down on the top step of the porch.

Sam and Emily joined him, both acting unsettled, as if unsure of what to do or say. Charlotte could tell they were more excited than they let on, but they also didn't want to seem uncool in front of Jordan.

"Grandma, do you think I can take a few photos?" Emily asked.

Charlotte looked to Tracy, who nodded her approval.

"Yes, but remember not to get in anyone's way," Charlotte encouraged, trying to turn the conversation back to a more positive note. "These good people have a job to do."

The men with the camera equipment moved toward the barn, and Charlotte watched as they propped open both front barn doors and set up two large lights outside. They hooked them up to an outside outlet, flooding the barn with light and most likely scaring the barn cats, which scampered about. Everyone seemed to be in motion.

Christopher was especially interested in all the cameras and how they worked, and he tagged along, close enough to watch what was happening but not too close.

Every few minutes, Emily lifted her camera to her eye, focused, and snapped a shot. Charlotte smiled as she noted that Sam and Jordan actually looked interested and that Christopher became even more involved when the guys started asking questions about the farm, questions Christopher was eager to answer. She watched as he chatted with one of the prop guys near the garden, pointing out and explaining what the different plants were.

With Christopher occupied, Toby paced back and forth among the house, the barn, and the trucks, sniffing people, equipment, and vehicles as she tried to figure out what was going on.

Charlotte watched curiously as a group of men directed Pete to start up a tractor and drive it out to the horse pasture. She held back a chuckle as she imagined what Pete would think about driving back and forth in the pasture while they filmed him. A spurt of laughter burst from her lips as she also imagined Pete having to go to makeup and wardrobe.

Pete drove around the field for a while, but it didn't last long. Thirty minutes later the tractor was parked, and Pete was heading to his apartment to change into his overalls.

"I have to get to my chores," he mumbled, striding by.

"Pete doesn't seem too excited about them being here." Jordan shook his head.

"Well, Pete doesn't do well with change." Charlotte said. "He's used to the days passing just like they always do. In fact, I can think of only a few times he's even left Nebraska. Speaking of which, what do you think of our state, Jordan?" She looked into Jordan's face, trying to remember seeing him at Denise's funeral. She knew he'd been there, but she didn't remember much about that day except trying to comfort her grandchildren.

He shrugged. "Well, Nebraska's okay, I suppose. A lot different from San Diego. I never guessed I'd be in the middle of something like this, but I suppose it will be cool to see a singer at work."

"This isn't commonplace? But you live in California."

Charlotte shielded her eyes from the sun to look into his face. "Aren't there a lot of famous people there?"

"Actually, this one time—"

"Charlotte?" Will strode up, interrupting Jordan. "We were wondering if Bob has any more heavy extension cords around here. We need to set up lights by Trudy's stall."

"Well, I'll see what I can find in a minute." She turned back to Jordan. "What were you saying?"

He waved a hand at her. "No, go ahead. I'll tell you about my one and only movie star experience later. These people need help."

"You can say that again." Will slapped his leg and laughed. "But for now an extension cord will do."

Charlotte laughed and rose from her place on the porch. "Why don't I call my husband and see where those cords are."

"No need to call him. Here he comes." Emily pointed down the gravel road.

Charlotte glanced around the farm at all the people and all their supplies, and immediately her stomach tensed. Sure, it was Bob who had said they could come, but she wondered what his attitude would be now that they were all here.

She waved as she walked to the road where he parked, forcing a smile onto her face.

Chapter Fourteen

Charlotte had called Bob three times, and he still hadn't come in for lunch. She marched outside and found him encircled by a group of guys.

On the outside he appeared calm. He was sharing stories about the farm—about the time he delivered a calf in a blizzard and the recent tornado that had touched down—but Charlotte could tell that on the inside Bob wasn't at ease. His arms were crossed over his chest, and his fists were balled tightly. Even as he talked, his eyes weren't on the faces of his listeners. Instead, his gaze moved around the farm as he took in where everyone was and what each one was doing.

Charlotte hadn't heard him complain this time as she had when they'd hosted an open house for being named Adams County Farm of the Year. Then again, he hadn't had much time to worry about it or complain. Everything had happened so fast. Still, that didn't mean the reality of all these people on the farm was easy for Bob.

Charlotte approached, trying not to interrupt.

"So, would it be possible to get some tape of the combine harvesting?" Buck asked.

Bob chuckled. "Well, no. The crops aren't ready yet. We have another month or so before it's time to harvest."

"And we couldn't fake it?" Buck asked.

"Oh, you could fake it, but it'll ruin my crop and my machine in the process." Bob's voice was stern, and Buck nodded and walked away.

Seemingly unfazed, Bob turned his attention back to the cameraman and pointed out the best angle to get a good shot of both the front porch and the barn. As he spoke, Will approached and listened, jotting notes in a small notepad.

Charlotte stood by and listened for a while, hoping Bob would get the hint that she wanted to talk to him. Then she finally gave up and placed a hand on his arm. "Would you like me to bring your lunch out to you?"

"Do you have enough food for everyone, Char? We can't let our guests go hungry, now can we?"

Charlotte raised an eyebrow, looking around at the numerous people and tried to calculate how she'd pull off lunch for everyone. The thing was, she knew Bob wasn't offering to be hospitable. He was offering because he wanted to be able to eat *and* keep an eye on everyone.

Will raised his hands. "Oh, no worries here. A caterer from town should be out any minute. She came highly recommended and she's bringing us all lunch."

"Is it Mel from Mel's Place?" Bob asked. "She has the best food in town."

"Yes, I think that sounds right. You're welcome to join us."

"Thanks, but no thanks. What I meant to say . . ." Bob straightened his shoulders. "Is that Mel's food is second only to my wife's. I'll be back out in thirty minutes or so, and then we can talk about the type of paint you need for those fuel tanks."

"They're painting the fuel tanks?" Charlotte placed a hand over her heart. "Did you tell them that repainting those has been on your honey-do list for at least three years?"

Charlotte glanced at the two fuel tanks not far from the barn. One tank stored diesel for the tractors and the other had regular gas for the trucks and other farm machines. They were old and rusted, and had to be repainted every ten years or so.

"No, but now that you mention it, maybe I should give them the other items on the list too." Bob was trying to be lighthearted, but she could tell from the look in his eyes that he was worried about what type of job they'd do painting the fuel tanks. Bob opened his mouth to say something; then he turned toward the house, and Charlotte walked by his side, wondering what to say, how to help.

They'd almost made it to the house when a shout split the air. It was a man's voice, followed by cursing.

Charlotte turned around to find Britney saddled up and galloping through the front yard. A muscular man, dressed in tight Levi's and a vest but no shirt, was chasing her. Two other guys, including Buck, were chasing the guy and the horse.

"What's going on?" Bob shouted, and for the first time his calm exterior broke.

Buck paused and turned, catching his breath. Giving up the chase, he wandered over to Bob and Charlotte. "We were, uh, trying to get some shots for the video, and the horse went crazy, knocking our actor to the ground."

"Who gave you permission to use my horse . . . to saddle her up?" Bob tried to control his voice, but Charlotte could hear the quiver of anger lacing his words.

In the distance, she watched as the two guys caught Britney and led her back toward the horse pasture by her lead. Charlotte was just about to head in that direction to offer a hand when Emily jogged around the corner of the barn, running toward them.

"Emily, do you know what's going on? It's not like Britney to act like that. Was anyone hurt?"

"It's not Britney's fault. They kept following her with the truck and camera thing, and it scared her. Besides, they didn't even saddle her up right!"

Emily's face was white, and Charlotte reached a hand toward her, pulling her granddaughter close.

Buck turned toward Emily, pointing a finger at her face. "Listen, little girl, my dad trained horses for years and . . ."

"Wait a minute." Bob lifted his hands, stepping between Buck and Emily. "Don't talk to my granddaughter that way. Emily, go ahead and go inside. I'll take care of this."

"But Grandpa—"

"Emily, I said I'd take care of it."

Emily trudged up the porch steps and glanced back one last time before going inside and slamming the door.

Bob turned back to Buck. Bob towered over the man, and Charlotte was sure she'd never seen her husband's face so red. "Shouldn't someone have talked to me about my horse? That horse used to belong to my daughter; she means a lot to us."

"Actually, Bob, it was in that contract you signed. I just

assumed you'd read it. The contact says you've given us permission to use everything on the farm we might need for the making of the video."

"Yes, but we assumed that meant our shovel and our hay bales, not our horses."

"Well . . ." Buck let his voice trail off and he shrugged. Charlotte reached out and touched Bob's arm, reminding him to stay calm.

"As you know, my son is a lawyer, and I'm going to talk to him about that contract. Things are getting out of hand—fast."

"What are you saying, Mr. Stevenson?" Buck folded his arms over his chest. "That you're trying to back out? That you've changed your mind?"

"I'm saying . . ." Bob leaned in close, peering into Buck's eyes. ". . . that I'm going to talk to my son about my options." And with that he turned and marched up the porch steps and into the house, letting the door slam behind him.

"Grandma!" Christopher's voice split the air. "There are some people in here taking your stuff!"

Charlotte turned and noticed Tracy walking out of the house with some of her old milk bottles that had been displayed on a high shelf. She placed them on the porch next to the rocking chair and then hurried back inside. Through the kitchen window she could see Tami removing her curtains.

Charlotte hurried into the house. As if not knowing what to do, Sam and Jordan sat at the dining room table and seemed to watch the women in disbelief. Emily was looking out the window, focusing on what was happening in the horse pasture.

Charlotte approached the two women. "May I help you?"

"Yeah, can you tell me where your iron and ironing board are?" Tracy glanced around as if expecting them to materialize out of thin air. "I need to iron some clothes for Shae Lynne and some curtains for the window."

"You got new curtains for the window?"

"Yes, bright white ones. They're adorable. I hope you don't mind," Tami said with a smile. "It will really brighten the view from the porch."

Charlotte didn't know what to say. "I, uh, suppose that's okay just as long as I can put the old ones back up when you're through. Those were Bob's mom's curtains, and the windows wouldn't be the same without them."

"Oh, yeah, I'll leave them in the laundry room—if you want to put them back up." From the look on Tracy's face Charlotte could tell that she thought putting the old curtains back was a bad idea.

"We're just going to use the new ones, you know, for the video." Tami explained. "I assumed you'd want to keep them because they're white and bright."

Charlotte didn't have time to respond before Emily rushed up to her. "Grandma, Britney keeps running away." She pointed out the window. "I think she's scared of that man. He's just so big and scary looking."

"Well, your Grandpa's upstairs talking to Uncle Bill on the phone. I'm sure when he's off the phone he'll take care of it—one way or the other."

"What does that mean?" Emily's lips puckered into a

frown. "He's not going to cancel the contract, is he?" Emily grabbed Charlotte's arm. "Grandma, don't let him do that. I *have* to meet Shae Lynne. I just have to."

"Do you, now?" Charlotte patted her granddaughter's hand. "But I didn't think you liked them being there, scaring Britney like that."

Emily bit her lip. "It's not that I don't want them to be here. Don't you think Grandpa could just talk to them? Tell them how to take care of her?"

"We'll see. Why don't we just let your grandpa handle this. I think that either way he'll make the right decision."

Emily didn't argue, but she returned to the window with a scowl.

Sam rose and motioned to Jordan.

Charlotte turned to them, anticipating their complaints. "And what about you two?" She placed her hands on her hips.

Sam just shook his head. "We're heading into town to the rec center to play some Ping-Pong and maybe go to Jenny's Creamery to get some shakes."

Jordan crossed his arms over his chest. "Things are getting a little too intense around here."

"Can I go?" Emily asked Charlotte. "I don't want to stay and watch. I can't take it either way."

"Sure, do you mind taking Christopher too?" Charlotte hurried to her purse to get some money for their snack.

"Yeah, I'll ask him if he wants to go." Sam grabbed a soda from the fridge, and Jordan did the same.

Charlotte handed them some money, and Sam, surprised, didn't complain about taking his younger siblings along. "Do you know what time you'll be home?"

Sam shrugged. "Why don't you call and tell us when these people leave, and then we'll let you know." Then he and the other kids scrambled out to squeeze into Sam's little car.

As if sensing the tension, Tami and Tracy put down the curtains and walked out of the kitchen, stepping onto the porch.

Charlotte sighed. Outside, Buck was once again trying to get the actor on Britney, and upstairs she could hear Bob's booming voice as he talked with Bill.

Will they let us back out? Is it too late to change our minds?

Charlotte sighed again. Nothing seemed worth all this conflict. Not even Shae Lynne.

Chapter
Fifteen

Y ou want me to touch what?"

Early Tuesday morning Jordan sat on the three-legged stool at Trudy's side and stared at her teats. He was wearing an old pair of Pete's overalls that were four inches too short. Sam attempted to hold in a chuckle at the sight of his friend sitting on the stool with his pant legs high above his ankles.

"Watch." Sam reached down and ran his hand down from Trudy's swollen udder to the top of a teat that was enlarged and full of milk. Then with a smooth, quick motion he moved his hand downward, squeezing out the milk.

"Dude. That's disgusting. I'm not going to grab the cow's . . . you know." He pushed the stool back and stood. "Don't you have another chore I can help with? Anything, please."

Sam pushed his baseball cap back from his face and eyed the barn. He pretended to be thinking hard to find something for Jordan to do, but the truth was he knew exactly what chore to give his friend.

Sam shrugged, "Well, I suppose you could muck out the stalls."

"Sure, anything. What's that?"

Sam took a pitchfork from where it hung on two nails. "You have to get that wheelbarrow and go to each stall, scooping out the waste and shoveling it into the wheelbarrow."

"The waste? Like in . . ."

"Yes, dung. Manure. It's not too bad really. Unless you want to try milking again?"

"No thank you." Jordan lifted his hands in surrender. "I think mucking, or whatever it's called, will work for me."

Sam sat at Trudy's side and began to milk her, slower than he usually did. Out of the corner of his eye he watched as Jordan moved the wheelbarrow toward one of the empty stalls. He attempted to pinch his nose with one hand as he scooped the dung with the other. When that didn't work he applied both hands to the pitchfork and set to work with gusto.

Sam smiled, knowing that this story would be retold in San Diego to everyone Jordan came across. Sam smirked at that thought. *At least he'll have something exciting to talk about. And I won't have to muck any stalls today.*

SAM TOOK A BITE out of his large stack of pancakes, thinking that next time he should go to San Diego instead of Jordan coming here. Things would be so much simpler that way. Who knew life on a farm could be so complicated?

Jordan sat beside Sam, shoveling pancakes into his mouth, telling Grandma over and over again how wonderful they were.

"I'm glad you're enjoying them." Grandma chuckled.

"I know breakfast always tastes better after a busy morning doing chores."

Grandpa poured himself some coffee and sat next to Sam. "So you guys going to the parade this morning?"

Sam shrugged. "I don't know. We haven't talked about it."

"Oh, you need to go. The fair parade is like the ultimate small-town-America thing to do." Grandma scooped another pancake onto Jordan's plate.

Sam wrinkled his nose.

Grandpa elbowed him, almost causing him to poke his fork into his cheek. "I know you think this stuff is dumb, or—how do you say it? lame?—but Jordan might think it's cool." Grandpa looked around Sam to meet Jordan's gaze. "After the parade they have a tractor pull that's fun to watch."

Jordan almost choked on the orange juice he was drinking, and Sam rolled his eyes.

"Yeah, that does sound cool. We should go, Sam." Jordan had a smirk on his face that told Sam he was just saying that to be nice.

"Can I go?" Christopher asked, putting down his Game Boy. "I want to see the fair again."

Emily's footsteps could be heard coming down from upstairs. "Go where?"

"Sam and Jordan are going to the parade and then the tractor pull. Do you want to go?"

"Sure, I'll go." Emily walked into the kitchen and grabbed an apple from the counter, taking a big bite.

"But what about the video?" Charlotte asked. "Are they coming back today?"

"Of course they'll come. Do you think they'll just leave all their stuff?" Sam pointed out the window. There was equipment everywhere, which he was sure didn't make Grandpa very happy.

"Sam, you know what I mean. Grandma, are they going to finish the video?" Emily hesitated as if she were afraid of the answer. "Is Shae Lynne going to be here?"

"Bob, do you want to tell the kids?" Grandma placed her coffee cup on the table and tilted her head.

"Well, after a long talk with Bill and another one with Buck, I've decided they can come today and do some more shots, but they really didn't tell us when Shae Lynne would be here, except that it probably wouldn't be today."

"So they're continuing?" Emily asked.

"At least for today. I need a chance to talk to Buck and Will again. I want to make sure we're all on the same page today—that we treat each other with respect."

"Okay, I think I'll go with you." Emily turned to Sam.

"Yeah, me too," said Christopher.

IN TOWN, THEY DECIDED to park at the fairgrounds.

"Do you want to take our skateboards?" Sam asked.

Jordan looked around, eyeing the fairgrounds and the people all around him. "Maybe later. I want to check out this parade first . . . you know, just in case your grandpa asks."

With Emily and Christopher trailing behind them, the boys walked down to Lincoln Street.

Sam was looking for a place to sit when he spotted someone waving from across the street. Looking closer, he realized it was Uncle Pete and Miss Simons.

"Hey look, they have a spot over there." Sam pointed, and they hurried across the street just before the first ambulance drove by slowly clearing the parade route with its lights flashing and siren blaring.

"Is there room?" Sam asked, looking at their narrow strip of curb space.

"Sure there is." Pete patted his side, and Miss Simons scooted over, cuddling next to him. Pete smiled awkwardly. Emily and Christopher occupied the space she'd been sitting in, and Jordan and Sam stood behind them.

"Do you have parades like this near you?" Dana asked, glancing back over her shoulder at Jordan.

"Well, there's the Rose Parade up in Pasadena. Maybe you've seen it on TV?" Jordan paused as he watched some high schoolers walk by pulling pigs in wagons that had been decorated to look like homes of straw, sticks, and bricks. "But, uh, no," Jordan continued. "Our parades are really nothing like this."

Jordan pulled his digital camera from his pocket and looked like he might actually be interested. He even snapped a few shots of a clown who was handing out candy to all the little kids.

A float carrying Future Farmers of America was followed by some old-fashioned cowboys on horseback. Sam was just about to suggest they retrieve their skateboards from his car when the shrill of a fire engine's siren filled the air.

As the fire truck came into view carrying Smokey the Bear, Jordan elbowed Sam's ribs . . . hard.

"Hey, what was that about?" Sam complained.

"No way! It's Smokey!" Jordan called out. He pulled out

his camera again. "Dude, I've only seen him on TV before." Jordan snapped a shot, and Sam wasn't sure if he was actually excited or just being sarcastic. "I remember when I was five I wanted to meet Smokey the Bear. My mom took me to the zoo, and I cried the whole time. I wanted to meet the bear with the ranger's hat. You know, the one that fought forest fires."

Laughter burst from Sam's lips. "I didn't know that."

"Yeah." Jordan shrugged. "I didn't tell anyone that a bear had been my secret idol." Jordan grinned. "Cool."

After that, Jordan seemed to get more into the parade, and Sam let himself relax and enjoy it too.

A section of floats came next—mostly 4-H groups trying to outdo each other—and then the marching band and a senior citizens dance club that broke out in square dancing right in front of them.

"So that's your school band?" Jordan asked, pointing to the two dozen band members performing music for the square dancers.

Sam smirked and pointed to the old ladies in their big skirts. "Yes, and those are our cheerleaders."

Laughter burst from Jordan's lips, and Sam joined him. The laughter continued through the ponies dressed up as pigs and the tractors carrying the fair queen and her court.

"At least they're having a good time," Dana commented to Pete, looking over her shoulder at them.

"And are you?" Pete asked.

"Yes, I love the parade and everything about the fair."

"Know what could make it better?" Pete brushed a strand of hair off his shoulder.

"What?"

Pete grabbed a piece of candy off the roadway in front of them that the little kids had somehow missed. "Candy for my girlfriend."

Dana scowled, then took the candy, playing along. "Ah, Pete, you're too sweet. I've always wanted a piece of candy just like this." She playfully slugged his shoulder.

"Just something sweet for my sweet." Pete smirked.

Sam looked at Jordan, and when their eyes met they started laughing again. He never would call Uncle Pete romantic. Yet seeing them made Sam wonder about Arielle. Was she around here somewhere? He hadn't talked to her since Sunday. He still hadn't told Arielle about Shae Lynne's video being filmed at the farm. He figured if everyone else knew then she probably knew too.

Sam hoped they'd have a chance to hang out with Arielle and Natalie this afternoon. That should make Jordan happy.

The roar of engines interrupted Sam's thoughts, and Jordan tugged on his arm. "No way, are you serious? Monster trucks?"

Jordan started snapping photos again with a huge smile on this face, and for the first time Sam believed his friend *was* enjoying himself.

"I'm pretty sure they'll be parked over at the fair," Pete said. "They even let you climb up and look inside if you like."

"Oh man, that would be awesome."

Sam was chuckling to himself over Jordan's excitement when he felt small, soft hands covering his eyes.

"Guess who," a soft voice whispered into his ear. Sam's

heart pounded. He gently took the hands from his eyes and then twisted around, peering into Arielle's face.

More sirens passed and Sam had to almost shout to be heard. "Hey, I was hoping to see you here!"

Arielle smiled. "I called your house and your Grandma said you'd be here!" She shouted back. Natalie was with her, smiling up at Jordan with a grin that almost matched her cousin's.

"Well, the parade is almost over. Do you want to head over to the fairgrounds and walk around together?" Arielle asked.

"Sure," Jordan answered before Sam had a chance.

Sam turned to Christopher and Emily. "We're going to the fairgrounds for a while."

"Yeah, fine. I'm sure we'll see you around." Emily didn't even look up as she was texting someone on her phone.

"We're going to go on rides!" Christopher exclaimed. "Well, Dylan and I are anyway. And we're going to put our money together to see how big of a stuffed animal we can win on the games!"

"Sounds like a party." Sam nodded, taking Arielle's hand in his.

They walked back to the fairgrounds, and Jordan entertained everyone with stories about California. The girls couldn't seem to get enough, especially Natalie.

"Do you ever see movie stars?" Natalie asked, scooting closer to Jordan as they walked.

"Yeah, of course. Last year a friend and I went up to Hollywood with his uncle who was visiting. We were just hanging out, checking the stars on the sidewalk—you know the ones with everyone's names on them—and I looked up to see Keanu Reeves walking in my direction."

"No way!" Arielle gasped. "He's one of my favorite actors. Even though it's a really old movie, I love *The Matrix*."

"Oh yeah, and *Speed*," Natalie added, touching Jordan's arm.

People pressed all around them, and Sam snickered at how caught up the girls were in Jordan's words. He'd already heard this story, and it seemed the girls were more impressed than he'd been. Still, as Sam looked around at all the ordinary people, he couldn't imagine what it would be like to look up and actually see a movie star walking toward you. A famous singer is one thing, but someone who made a lot of movies and a lot of money would be even more impressive.

"So did you talk to him? Talk to Keanu?" Natalie asked.

"Well, he was with this woman, and they stopped to buy movie tickets at the theater. I walked up and touched his arm—just to say hi—and this crowd of people realized who he was and rushed forward."

"A crowd?" Sam smirked. Last time Jordan told this story it hadn't been a crowd but rather two rappers who'd been trying to sell their CDs on the street.

"Yeah, there were people rushing forward trying to talk to him, and I kinda got pushed to the side."

"But at least you touched him," Natalie sighed. "I've never touched anyone famous." She grabbed Jordan's hand. "But now I've touched someone who's touched someone famous."

Arielle laughed, and Sam shook his head. He leaned

close to Arielle's ear as they walked. "I think she just wanted to hold his hand. She's not letting go."

Arielle glanced up at Sam and nodded. "You think?"

Once inside the fairgrounds, Jordan attempted not to seem too impressed by their simple country ways, but the more they walked around, the more excited he became.

"Hey look, a mechanical bull. Do you want to watch me ride it?"

"I'd love to watch you." Sam crossed him arms over his chest.

"You going to try?" Jordan asked as he took out his wallet to pay for the ride.

"Are you kidding? I'd rather buy a corn dog than pay to get thrown on my butt."

"They have corn dogs here?" A smile lit up Jordan's face. "After this ride, my treat. Corn dogs all around."

Sam crossed his arms again as Jordan climbed onto the mechanical bull.

"I can't believe he's doing it." Arielle covered her mouth with her hand.

"Go, Jordan!" Natalie clapped her hands.

A guy in a cowboy hat helped Jordan get settled on the mechanical bull and gave him a strap to hold.

The bull started slowly. "Yahoo!" Jordan laughed, waving his free hand in the air as the machine started to spin and jerk.

"So, how's it going?" Arielle asked. "You know, are things different with you and Jordan than they were in California? I mean—"

Jordan's yelp interrupted Arielle's words, and Sam looked up in time to see his friend flying through the air, all arms and legs. He landed on the padded ground with a thump amid the girls' screams of laughter. Natalie ran over to help him up, and Sam couldn't help but laugh too, especially over the fact that Jordan had no idea how much country he'd be colliding with over the next few days.

"Everything's good," Sam replied and smiled at Arielle.

As he said it he could see from Jordan's face that their disagreement on Saturday had been forgotten.

"Dude, that was the best thing ever!" Jordan exclaimed, brushing himself off.

"Yeah, he'll be repeating that story soon," Arielle said, leaning in to speak into Sam's ear.

"Totally." Sam squeezed her shoulder. "Come on. I believe we were promised corn dogs."

Jordan couldn't stop talking about the ride as they stood in line at the carnival food booth. They were just about to order when Sam heard the sounds of his friends' voices. He turned around to see Jake and Paul approaching.

"Hey, Sam, Jordan," Paul called, waving.

"Make that six corn dogs," Jordan said, paying the lady.

As they ate their corn dogs, Paul and Jake talked about the tractor pull. They were just tossing their corn-dog sticks into the large trash bin when Jake's eyes brightened as he remembered something. "Oh, man, that's what I was going to ask you. We need two more people to help with the pig wrestling. You guys interested?"

"Pig wrestling?" Jordan took his last bite, wiped the mustard from his lips, and stepped closer. "That sounds even better than the mechanical bull."

Chapter
Sixteen

Emily glanced toward the entrance to the fairgrounds and watched the lines of people heading inside. Everyone was in a group and happy to be there. She was neither. Christopher had met up with Dylan and his mom and was probably going on every ride possible.

Her only hope was that Ashley could meet up with her. When Ashley didn't answer her cell phone, Emily called Mel's Place.

It took five rings before someone picked up the phone.

"Mel's Place," said a tired voice that Emily recognized as Ashley's mom's.

"Hi, Mrs. Givens. This is Emily. Can Ashley talk?"

The noise of the diner filled the phone. "Emily, thank goodness you're not another call-in order. If I get one more . . ." Then, realizing who she was talking to, her voice calmed. "Actually Ashley is running an order for me. Can I have her call you back?"

"Yes. I mean, okay, I just thought we could meet at the fair. I'm over here right now. I know she's been busy . . ."

"I know, poor Ashley. I'll pass the word, but I doubt she can head over to the fair today. I do know she was planning on going to the barrel races tomorrow though—Ginger! No, that order is for the gentleman waiting by the back door. Yes, I told you it was a to-go order. Anyway, Emily, I'm sorry Ashley hasn't been able to do much, but she's looking forward to the barrel races, and she can even stay at your house afterward if—no, Ginger, the coffee is for table four."

Emily listened as Melody directed more orders, and just when she was sure Mrs. Givens had forgotten she was on the line, the harried woman continued the conversation.

"Okay, sweetie, I've gotta run. I'll have Ashley call you. Enjoy the day." Mrs. Givens's voice trailed off, and then she hung up.

Great. Just great. Nothing was worse than walking around the fair and looking like a total loser, with a capital L.

But that's what she did for a while, glad she'd brought her camera. It made her feel like she wasn't a complete dork, hanging out all alone. Instead, she wandered around taking photos of the people at the fair—the cowboy with a black vest and a cell phone hanging off his belt, the 4-H girls combing out their cows' tails, and all the parents laughing at the wide grins on their children's faces as they rode the mini-motorcycles around the track—and around and around.

The sky was overcast, providing a slight barrier from the sun's rays, but it still didn't do much for the heat. The air was thick and muggy, and it carried on it the aromas of all the greasy fair food. Emily's stomach turned; she'd do anything for a cool ocean breeze like they used to get in San Diego.

"Emily!" She turned to find her Aunt Anna coming toward her with Jennifer and Madison.

"Hi, Aunt Anna." She waved. "Hi, guys." Emily squatted

down and gave her cousins a hug. They were dressed in matching denim skirts and adorable red button-up blouses. Both of them had their hair in pony tails and red bows.

"Emily! Emily!" They squeezed her neck so hard it was hard for her to breathe.

Emily stood. "So what are you guys up to?"

"We rode the horses on the carousel." Jennifer's face shone.

"And the ponies." Madison clapped her hands.

Anna placed a hand on her hip. "Yes, they loved it. Even though it really doesn't make sense to me. We paid five dollars for them to go around in a circle for five minutes when they could ride a horse at Grandpa's house for free."

"So what are you doing?" Anna looked into Emily's face with an expectant smile. "Jennifer wanted me to go on the Scrambler with her, but I told her I can't." Anna rubbed her stomach that showed the smallest baby bump. "You know, pregnant mommies aren't allowed on those rides."

Emily's heart fell, noticing the hopeful look on her cousins' faces. She loved both of them, but the last thing she wanted was to spend all afternoon riding on the kiddie rides. As she was trying to think of a good excuse, Emily looked up and noticed Arielle and Natalie walking toward her. Her heart pounded.

"Arielle!" Emily called.

Arielle wandered over. "Emily! Hi, Mrs. Stevenson. Hi, girls. This is my cousin Natalie. What are you doing today? Are you having fun at the fair?"

"I rode on a pony," Jennifer exclaimed.

"And we're going to go on rides," Madison added. "Maybe Emily will go with us."

Emily eyed Arielle and Natalie. "Actually, I was going to spend time with my friends. Right, Arielle?" Emily nodded enthusiastically.

"Yeah, uh, we're going to hang out. Sam and the guys are watching the tractor pull, so we're going to check out some of the displays and stuff."

"But, Emily, can't you just go on a few rides? Jennifer has been waiting all year." Anna wore a smile, but Emily could tell she wasn't happy that Emily wasn't cooperating with her plan.

Emily glanced over at the line of people waiting for the Scrambler. It was a forty-five-minute wait at least. Not to mention her stomach didn't feel great. One thing was sure, "County Fair" would never be made into an air-freshener fragrance. The smells of animals, fried food, and sweaty people made Emily's stomach turn just thinking about all of it.

"Why don't you try to find Christopher?" Emily encouraged her cousins. "He loves those kinds of rides. He's wandering around here somewhere with his friend Dylan. And maybe I'll see you later."

Anna rubbed her stomach again, and her forced smile turned into a scowl. "That's it. That's all you're going to say?"

Emily shrugged, not knowing what else to do. She bit her lip and turned to Arielle, seeking backup.

Arielle crossed her arms over her chest, unsure of what to do and say. Natalie fidgeted awkwardly.

"Okay, if you really don't have time . . ." Anna let the last word drag out. "You know, after this I was thinking I might stop by the farm for the video shoot, but the way things are turning out, it seems like everyone has their own plans."

"Well, I don't know. You should call Grandma. She always loves when you visit."

Anna nodded an acknowledgment, but she didn't say anything else. As she walked away, Emily could hear her promising a balloon for each girl since they couldn't go on the rides they wanted.

Emily felt bad, but she also knew she couldn't handle standing in that line in this heat. She also knew she probably couldn't handle the ride either.

"Okay, I'm totally confused." Arielle confessed as she and Natalie watched Anna and the girls walk away. "Were we supposed to meet up and do something?"

Emily laughed. "No, sorry. I just knew if I didn't make a quick escape I would end up spending all my time on the kiddie rides. And for some reason that doesn't sound fun at all."

"Yeah, well, we do have a little while to hang out. We're supposed to be meeting Sam and the guys again a little later."

"Cool. I've just been walking around and taking photos."

"Oh yeah, I saw the ones you entered. Congratulations."

"Congratulations? For what?"

"For your ribbons. It looked like you did really well."

"Really? I thought they weren't going to be judged until the end of the week. You know, after the fair."

"No. They do it the first day. Right after they're entered. Do you want to go over and look? We'll walk with you."

"Sure." Emily swung her camera case on her shoulder

and couldn't help but smile as they entered the arts and crafts barn.

"Look, they're over here." Arielle pointed to a wall that said YOUTH OPEN CLASS. Sure enough, there were two of her prints with blue ribbons hanging from them. She felt her chest warm and all the cares of the day seemed to disappear.

"Wow. I didn't expect blues . . . but I only see two of them here. Did you see another one?"

"Are you Emily Slater?" a voice said behind her.

Emily turned and noticed an older woman standing there with bright red lips and a wide smile.

"Yes, ma'am."

"Well, we moved your photo . . . it's the one with the sunflower. It's over there on that wall."

Emily looked to where she was pointing and noticed the wall by the door said BEST OF SHOW. There, in the middle of them all, was her framed print of the sunflower with a large purple ribbon.

"What's it doing over there?" Emily asked in disbelief.

She stepped closer, noticing the ribbon read BEST IN YOUTH DIVISION.

"This is where we put all of our top winners. You should be proud, young lady. Some people have entered for years and years and have never won this."

The woman went on talking about Emily's grandparents. She talked about how she'd gone to school with Grandpa Bob and how Emily must have gotten some of her grandmother's talents in her genes. Emily nodded, but she didn't answer. She was hardly listening. Her mind was just focused on that ribbon. Her fingers tightened around the strap of the camera case. She couldn't wait to call her grandma and let her know.

Emily's thoughts were interrupted by the sound of a voice from the other side of the partition. "Yeah, she thinks she's cool, but I heard from Nora, the girl at Kepler's who developed the photos, that Emily didn't even take the pictures. I heard her Uncle Pete did it, and she's taking all the credit."

Emily recognized the voice. She didn't have to walk to the other side to know it was Nicole. Meanwhile, the older woman next to Emily continued talking about all the new people who had entered this year, oblivious to the conversation happening nearby. Emily knew Arielle had heard Nicole because Emily felt the slightest touch of support on her arm.

Emily smiled at the lady. "That's so cool." She took a step back, hoping the lady got the idea. "I think I'll go call my grandma and tell her about the win."

Instead of letting Emily leave, the lady grabbed her arm. "Your grandparents aren't here? They're always at the fair." Then she nodded, remembering. "Oh yes, they have that video being filmed on their farm. I bet you're excited about that?"

Emily tensed, hoping Nicole didn't hear what the lady was saying. She didn't need anything else for Nicole to talk about.

"So have you had a hard time sleeping, knowing that a famous star is going to be on your farm?"

"Yeah, well—" Emily stuttered.

"You know, I usually don't go to concerts but I just might get tickets this year," the woman continued, "and see what this singer is all about."

"Great! Well, maybe we'll see you there." Arielle tugged on Emily's arm, pulling her out into the bright sunshine with Natalie following behind them.

"Have a great day," Arielle called over her shoulder.

They walked outside, and Emily took in a deep breath. Somehow in the last minute all the excitement she'd had from winning best of show was gone.

"Thanks for getting me out of there." Emily turned to Arielle. Her eyes watered from the sun. Or at least she tried to pretend the sun was the problem.

"Don't pay any attention to Nicole." Arielle wrapped her arm around Emily's shoulders. "She's just jealous because she entered lots of photos and only got one blue."

"Yeah, well, I don't know why she has to be so mean to me. We don't even hang out in the same groups."

Arielle's eyes lifted, and Emily knew without turning that Nicole had exited the building and was standing behind her.

Emily turned slowly.

"You talking about me?" Nicole asked. She was wearing jean shorts and a green T-shirt that read COUGARS on the front. Emily guessed that she'd be working at the cheerleaders' food booth later today.

"Only because you were talking about me first." She crossed her arms over her chest. "And for your information, I took those photos myself."

"Yeah, whatever. I was just saying that's what I heard. I didn't mean anything by it."

Nicole was with Lily Cunningham and another girl Emily recognized as another one of the cheerleaders, but before Emily could respond Nicole stomped away.

"See? She just didn't know," Arielle said, shrugging as if the words just exchanged made everything better.

"Well, I just don't understand what I ever did to her."

Arielle glanced at her watch, obviously finished with talking about Nicole. "Listen, Natalie and I are supposed to meet the guys over by the games. Sam promised to win me a big stuffed animal and I bet Jordan will try to win one for Natalie. Why don't you come along?"

Emily saw her grandma approaching in the distance. "Well, maybe I'll meet you over there. My grandma's here and I want to tell her about my ribbons."

"Okay, cool. Catch up with us later." Arielle and Natalie walked away, and Emily watched her grandma approach from the opposite direction.

"Hey, I was hoping I'd find you over here," Charlotte said. "I wanted to see how you did on your photographs."

Emily looked into her grandma's face, noticing that she looked tired and maybe a bit frustrated. Still, Grandma smiled as if trying to hide it. She always tried to act like everything was fine.

"I thought you weren't coming in to the fair until later." Emily tried to return her grandma's smile, knowing she did about as well at hiding her emotions as her grandmother did.

"Yes, well, I was getting a little overwhelmed by the video people too. When I left they were rearranging my living room and putting all my plants in front of the window, just in case they were taping the front porch and someone could see in through the window."

"Are you serious?" The look of frustration on her grandmother's face caused Emily to chuckle.

"So I thought I'd come in early and console myself with an elephant ear or a funnel cake—and see how you did on your photos." Grandma patted Emily's shoulder. "I'm glad I caught you before you went in. I didn't want you to be too disappointed. You need to remember that it's your first year. I can't think of many people who did great their first year out."

"Yeah, you can come see." Emily shrugged, trying to hide her smile. "Oh, but one thing first, what's an elephant ear?"

Grandma laughed. "Well, you're going to have to eat one and find out. It's actually like a large, flat doughnut that's similar to Indian bread. I love mine with powdered sugar and honey. Mmmm."

"Yeah, after the photos." She tried to force herself to be excited, but as Emily walked inside toward the open-class wall she couldn't shake Nicole's words.

"Emily, look at that!" Her grandma's face glowed with pride. "Two blue ribbons. I'm so proud of you."

Emily nodded. "Well, not all of them got blue ribbons." She turned and pointed to the wall by the front door.

Grandma turned and her hands covered her mouth. "Best of show? Emily Slater, did you get best of show?"

Emily followed her grandmother over to the wall. Grandma's fingers trailed down the antique frame and then touched the large, purple ribbon.

Her grandmother turned to her. "I don't understand. Why did you look so down?"

"Oh, mostly because of Nicole. I overheard her saying

that Uncle Pete was the one who took the photos, not me. And that I was trying to take all the credit."

"You know that's not the truth, right?"

"Yeah, of course."

"Then you need to not let it bother you."

Emily sighed. "Easier said than done."

"Can we talk for a minute?" Charlotte asked.

Emily followed her grandma outside, and they found an empty bench around the side of the arts and crafts building.

"You know, I understand what you're going through. You're not the only one that people have been talking about lately."

"Really?"

"Yes, I discovered that people have been talking about me too. Talking about how your grandfather and I think we're better than everyone else because Shae Lynne's shooting her video at our farm. They think we have all the luck."

"The *luck*? Have they been to the farm and seen what's going on?" Emily couldn't help but laugh.

"Well, that's the thing. Most of the time people's mouths are moving but they don't understand fully what's going on. Sometimes they're jealous. Most of the time they're uninformed. Lots of times they really just need to seal their lips."

Emily was surprised to hear her grandmother talking this way. "Yeah, but what are we supposed to do?"

"I've been thinking about this, knowing I was going to see some of those people again. I have to admit I did a bit of praying too."

Emily waited, studying her grandmother's face, looking for any sign of bitterness but not seeing any. "And?"

"And I realized I needed to forgive them for speaking out and to let it go."

"Just like that?"

"Well, if I were to hold on to all the mean, spiteful, or uncaring words that people have said over the years, I'd be a pretty bitter woman. And I don't want that. I don't want to be that type of person."

Emily watched the crowd walking by. Most of them had smiles on their faces as they expected a fun time. In a way, she'd been robbed of that feeling. And the good feelings about her win.

"Yeah, you're right. I'll try to do that. I'll try to forgive Nicole and to forget what she said."

Her grandmother patted her arm. "That's my girl. Now, I think we need to celebrate your win. How about getting that elephant ear?"

"Awesome! That sounds perfect to me!"

As Emily walked arm-in-arm with her grandma, she said a silent prayer that God would help her forgive Nicole. The sun seemed a bit brighter, and so did her heart.

CHARLOTTE WAS GLAD TO SEE that by the time she arrived home the video crew was gone for the day. She could tell that props had been moved. And she saw from the fresh paint on the fuel tanks that they'd been hard at work, but thankfully she'd missed all the drama.

Charlotte parked the car, and Emily and Christopher got

out. They both seemed tired from a day at the fair. Emily especially seemed happy to be home. Since Ashley hadn't been able to get off after all, Emily had volunteered in the church's pie booth with Charlotte. And while all the older ladies enjoyed having Emily there, Charlotte knew Emily didn't find the afternoon quite as enjoyable.

"Christopher, can you set the table for dinner? I'm going to make grilled-cheese sandwiches and tomato soup tonight—your favorite."

"Ah, Grandma." Christopher leaned down and picked up a stick. "I was going to work with Toby. I have one last night before the dog show." Sensing the young boy's presence, Toby barked and raced out from behind the barn, jumping up on Christopher and nearly leaping into his arms.

"I'll do it." Emily volunteered. Then she trudged up the porch steps. "I don't have anything else to do." She entered the house and let the door slam.

"Thanks," Charlotte called behind her.

"So, are you ready?" Charlotte turned to Christopher.

"Oh, yeah." Christopher tossed the stick, and Toby bounded after it. Then he smirked. "The problem is, is Toby ready?"

Charlotte laughed. "Yes, I guess that is the question of the evening."

After the simple dinner, Charlotte sat next to Bob on the living room sofa. Emily lay on the floor, watching a reality show, and even though it was nearly dark, Christopher was still outside working with Toby.

"Things go well today?" Charlotte asked Bob.

He turned the page in his paper. "Uh-huh."

"Did every one play nice?" She smiled at her own joke.

Bob didn't seem quite as amused. "Yes, Charlotte. It was fine. No problems." He turned another page.

"Well, aren't you going to ask how Emily did on her photography projects?"

Both Bob and Emily turned in her direction. Charlotte pointed at Emily. "Go ahead, tell him."

Emily sat up and crossed her legs. Then she shrugged. "Well, I got a couple of blue ribbons and . . . a best of show."

"Really?" Bob set his paper down. "A best of show?" He leaned forward in his seat. "On which picture?"

Emily smiled and turned down the volume on the television, pleased by her grandfather's interest.

"The one with the sunflower."

"Yeah, that is a good one."

"Toby . . . good girl." Christopher's voice carried in through the window.

Bob rose and patted Emily's head. Then he turned to the window. "Does Christopher compete tomorrow?"

"Yes, he's doing well." Charlotte rose and stood beside him.

Bob yawned and then unhooked his suspenders. "Can you believe that, Charlotte? Our grandchildren are getting ribbons at the fair. Just like my grandfather and father did. Just like I did, and their mother too. She would be so proud." Charlotte noticed the emotion in Bob's voice.

"Yes, she would, wouldn't she?" Charlotte slid down off the couch to kneel next to Emily on the floor. "Your mother would be proud," she said, tucking a strand of Emily's blonde hair behind her ear.

"Thanks, Grandma," Emily pressed her lips together. "I think I'll go with you tomorrow. You know, to cheer Christopher on. And to tell him what you just told me. Because I know she would be. Even if he doesn't win tomorrow, she'd be proud."

Chapter
Seventeen

Early Wednesday morning Charlotte sat in one of the folding chairs and glanced at her watch. Emily, Sam, and Jordan sat next to her, but Bob had decided to stay at the farm and keep an eye on the video shoot.

Christopher was going to be showing Toby in five minutes, and Charlotte hoped it didn't take too long. The bleachers weren't the most comfortable seats. In fact, her back was already starting to ache.

Charlotte noticed that they lined up the participants by age. Christopher was second in line, and he seemed so young compared to the others kids, mostly teens. He looked toward Charlotte, and she waved. He stood straight and tall but didn't smile.

Toby, on the other hand, didn't seem to be intimidated at all. Her tail wagged as she focused on the dog standing next to her. The large golden Lab seemed equally interested in Toby, sniffing her—much to the horror of his owner.

The judge stood before the group, explaining the rules. Charlotte took notes as the judge explained the five areas that Christopher and Toby would be judged on:

- Heel on leash and figure 8
- Stand for examination
- Recall
- Long sit (1 minute)
- Long down (3 minutes)

Charlotte was surprised that Christopher wouldn't be judged on some of the other things he'd worked on. She felt guilty for not paying attention. He'd focused on the hard stuff and hadn't spent that much time on the easier things.

Listen to the judge, Charlotte wanted to call out. Instead, Christopher kept looking at the dog, trying to get her to sit and leave the other dog alone.

"Come on, Christopher; pay attention," Emily whispered.

Thankfully, when it was time for Christopher to be judged, the other dogs were led out of the ring. Then, at the judge's command, Christopher aced heel on leash and figure 8. Then it was time for recall. Charlotte had seen Christopher practice this with Toby at least a hundred times on the front lawn. She just hoped that all that hard work would pay off.

Christopher stood straight and tall. He motioned to Toby. "Sit."

Christopher turned and started walking across the ring. Charlotte pressed her fingers to her lips. "Stay, Toby, stay," she whispered, her heart pounding.

Thankfully, Toby stayed.

Emily softly clapped her hands.

When Christopher finished crossing the ring he turned. The judge nodded, Christopher motioned, and Toby trotted across the ring as if she were an old pro at the showman-ship thing. The judge motioned again, and Christopher motioned for Toby to heel at his side. Instead, Toby cocked her head and licked Christopher's hand. Charlotte sighed, and she wondered if it was okay to pray for a dog to obey.

Charlotte saw the judge scribbling on his notepad and hoped Christopher would do better with the next round.

When Christopher was done with recall, Charlotte waited and watched for the other kids to compete. Some of them did great, and others . . . Well, it appeared as if they hadn't worked with the dogs at all.

After each participant had had a chance at the first three areas, the judge announced that the long sit and long down would be performed by the group of dogs in the ring.

All the dogs entered the ring, and again Toby's attention was drawn to the yellow Lab next to her.

"Focus, Toby," Charlotte muttered under her breath. "Don't be such a flirt."

"Yeah, Toby," Emily echoed. She pressed her fingers to her lips. Then to her closed eyelids, as if not wanting to watch.

"Okay, handlers, signal or command your dogs to sit and stay, and then join me in the center of the ring. Once here, turn and face your dogs."

"Sit," a unison of voices said. Then the whole group walked to the center. Toby watched Christopher and shiv-ered slightly as if wanting to follow him, but thankfully she stayed.

Charlotte had seen this event enough times to know that all the dogs were supposed to maintain the sit position with-out barking, whining, or moving from their spots. Once all the handlers turned and faced their dogs, the countdown began—one minute until they could be signaled to come and heel.

Toby glanced from Christopher to the yellow Lab, but thankfully she didn't move. When the minute was up, the judge ordered the handlers to walk back, circle their dogs, and then return to the heel position.

Charlotte blew out the breath she hadn't known she'd been holding.

"Only one more to go," the woman sitting next to Charlotte said.

"The hardest one," Emily added.

"Long down," Charlotte answered. "Who knew something so simple could be so tense?"

Charlotte folded and unfolded her hands on her lap. For the long down, at the handlers' command, the dogs had to assume the down position without assistance.

"Lie down. Down," Christopher told Toby.

Toby lay down, as did the other dogs. Then all the participants moved to the center of the ring. Christopher stood straight and tall. His lips moved slightly, and Charlotte guessed he was counting out the three minutes in his head. She looked at her watch, focusing as the minute hand went around once and then twice.

At the two-minute mark everything looked good, but it was the cock of Toby's head that told Charlotte something was up. Toby looked at Christopher and then at the yellow Lab again.

"Don't do it," Charlotte whispered.

"Come on, Toby." Emily sighed. "Only forty-five seconds left."

The yellow Lab whined, and Toby's tail wagged. Then,

with just a few seconds left, Toby crawled over to the lab and cuddled against his side. Even though Charlotte was horrified that Toby had moved, she couldn't help but laugh—as did the rest of the audience.

It wasn't until the laughter died down that Charlotte noticed Christopher in the center of the ring with his head down and his shoulders quivering. He was trying to hold in his emotion.

"Worked so hard, and foiled by a yellow Lab," Charlotte mumbled to herself.

Emily just shook her head, speechless.

The white ribbons were given out, followed by the reds and the blues. Charlotte, Emily, Sam and Jordan cheered loudly as the judge handed Christopher a red, but Charlotte could tell from his face that he was disappointed.

They were all waiting for him as he put Toby back on the leash and trudged out of the ring. Sam patted his shoulder. "Great job, bro."

"Yeah, I know I did great, but I can't believe Toby did that. I would have gotten a blue if she had stayed."

"I know, I know." Charlotte sighed.

"That's what love does to you." Emily giggled at her own joke.

"I wish that yellow Lab had never come."

"Well, I think it doesn't matter, because a red is pretty good in my book," Charlotte said. "Remember, it's your first time competing."

"My first and my last." Christopher stomped off. "Maybe next time I'll do a poultry project. Chickens don't fall in love, do they, Grandma?"

"I'm not sure, but let's not worry about that now. I need to take Toby home. Are you going to meet Dylan and his mom again?" Christopher nodded, but he didn't seem as excited about it as he had been earlier.

Sam and Jordan made a quick exit so they could get on to their day's events. "See you later, buddy," Sam said as he gave Christopher a high five.

Charlotte, Emily, Christopher, and Toby moved out of the building and tried to make their way through the crowd heading the other direction. It didn't help that every few steps someone stopped to admire Toby and pet her.

"Emily, did you want to ride back home with me, or stay here?"

Emily didn't have a chance to answer the question because just as they passed the hog barn Toby barked and lunged. The movement caught Christopher by surprise, and the leash slipped through his fingers.

"Toby, no!" Christopher shouted, chasing her.

Charlotte gasped, wondering what in the world had gotten into the dog. She didn't have to wonder long though, because as Charlotte hurried after both Toby and Christopher, she saw the swish of a yellow Lab's tail rounding the corner.

EMILY HAD TO ADMIT she was both frustrated and amused by Toby's disappearance. Frustrated, because they'd already spent thirty minutes searching the fairgrounds for her, and amused because Toby had a boyfriend. Emily smiled. *And in my opinion that yellow Lab is pretty cute too.*

Emily continued to push through the aisles of campers

and tents, peering under each one for the disappearing dogs. Finally she came across a large mobile home where the Lab's owner was hunkered down, calling his dog out from beneath the vehicle. Toby and her canine companion watched from the shadowed area under the vehicle but didn't seem interested in being found.

Emily hurried over. "Come on, girl. Come on, Toby," Emily called.

Grandma and Christopher joined them. Grandma called too, but neither dog budged.

"Toby knows she's in trouble," Grandma said.

"I'll try." Christopher hunkered down and held out his hand. "Come on, girl."

Toby's tail wagged, and then she trotted out to Christopher.

"She likes you best." Emily sighed.

Christopher petted Toby and slid on the leash.

"I'll take her from here," Grandma took the leash. "You're already late meeting up with Dylan."

"It's okay. I'll walk her to the car for you. Dylan will understand."

Emily followed Christopher and Charlotte.

"You stay with me," Christopher scolded Toby. Knowing she was in trouble, the dog stayed close to Christopher's side.

Emily couldn't help but notice the dejected look on her brother's face. His red ribbon dangled from his front belt loop, flapping like a sail without wind.

Grandma noticed his look too.

Emily looked at her grandma and then she approached

her brother. "You know, Christopher . . ." She placed a hand on his shoulder. "Mom would have thought this whole thing was cool." She softly laughed. "Except for the escaping part."

Christopher didn't comment. He just nodded and kicked at a rock in the roadway.

Grandma paused. "Emily, why don't you go back to the fair? I'll get Toby home, and then come back here. Christopher should go meet up with Dylan," she repeated again.

"Okay," Emily said, pausing and offering a quick wave. "Remember what I said, Christopher."

He nodded again, handed Toby over to Grandma, and offered Emily a bigger smile. "Thanks, Emily."

Since the guys were watching the second round of the tractor pull, Emily had planned to meet Arielle and Natalie again and cruise around the fairgrounds, looking for people they knew. She texted Arielle and they picked a meeting spot.

Once they met up they walked around for a while, and then sat near one of the stages and watched the Bedford High School band perform. When they tired of that, they walked around the animal barns, checking out the ribbons.

Emily smiled at the clucking of the chickens as they passed. She took a photo of the Nebraska flag waving in the wind. She smiled softly as she focused her camera and snapped a shot. It was turning out, she thought, to be a good day.

As Emily walked she realized that Grandma had been right in suggesting she try to forgive and forget the events of the previous day. She could have stayed mad and replayed the conversation with Nicole in her mind, but the day was better when she chose to do the opposite.

As Emily walked around with Arielle and Natalie, in a strange way the crowds of the fair reminded her of the crowds at Coronado Beach—especially at the Coronado Dell Resort near their home in San Diego. One of the fun things about going there was walking through the outside patio—and even the lobby—and pretending they belonged. They'd never been able to afford staying at such a place, but it was common for those hanging out at the beach to walk through the shops or get an ice cream in the small outdoor café.

The last time Emily was there, Mom had taken them ice skating in the small rink behind the large hotel. She had never understood how they kept it frozen, yet she enjoyed it all the same.

The rink was at the edge of the sandy beach, and ice skating while watching the large ships sail by on the Pacific Ocean had been one of her favorite things to do. In February, the Southern Californian sun shone as brightly as it did during summers in Nebraska, and they'd skated in T-shirts and jeans.

Like the crowds here at the fair, at the resort there had been old people on scooters and pouting, tired children who wanted one more ride, one more game, or one more treat.

Emily and Arielle had just settled down with half a watermelon, root beers, and snow cones when Nicole, Lily, and a girl whose nametag read KAITLIN approached. They'd been working in the school food booth, calling to everyone who passed to come get a hot dog or lemonade. Now their shift was over, and Emily wondered if yesterday's conversation was about to be repeated.

Nicole plopped down next to Arielle as if they were best friends.

"Hey, Arielle, is your dad patrolling the concert Friday night?"

Arielle narrowed her blue eyes in a distrusting gaze. "Yeah, why?"

"Oh, I was just wondering. Do you think he can let us slip backstage for just a few minutes so we can get our picture taken with Shae Lynne? I have a bet with my cousin in Colorado. I told her I can get a photo, and she says it's impossible."

"Yeah, my dad will be there, but the security backstage is going to be tight. They're not letting anyone near Shae Lynne—even the Stevenson farm will have security starting tomorrow."

"What do you mean? What's going on at the Stevenson farm?"

Arielle glanced at Emily. "Sorry. I thought everyone knew."

"Knew what?" Nicole scooted closer.

"Knew that Shae Lynne's next video is being taped at Sam and Emily's house."

Lily and Kaitlin turned in Emily's direction with mouths gaping.

"At Emily's house?" Nicole lifted her nose into the air. She laughed out loud. "That's a great joke."

The other girls didn't laugh.

"It's not a joke. I talked to Sam on the phone this morning. The video crew was there setting up." Arielle fixed her ponytail, rewrapping the rubber band around her dark hair.

Emily nodded, but Nicole still looked at her with disbelief.

"But has anyone actually seen Shae Lynne yet? Maybe they just said they were working with Shae Lynne." Nicole folded her arms over her chest.

Emily glanced at Arielle, seeking courage. "Uh, no. We haven't seen Shae Lynne, not yet, but she's supposed to be there tomorrow."

"Really?" Nicole's face brightened with a smile.

"Yeah, but they're not going to let anyone onto the property. Like Arielle said, there will be security and the whole thing is off limits."

"Who is it that's keeping everyone off limits?" Nicole scooted closer to Emily.

"You know, the video people."

"But it's your house. They can't stop you from inviting over a few friends, right?"

"Well, I guess not." Emily knew immediately what Nicole was asking, and with all of them looking at her she didn't know how to say no. "I suppose I can ask my grandma if it's okay if you all come and spend the night."

"Okay, sure." Nicole glanced at the others. "That will be cool. I've been wanting to stay over for a while."

Yeah, right. Emily nodded but didn't answer.

"Cool." Nicole jumped to her feet. "Do you want to go on some rides with us?"

Arielle shook her head. "No thanks. I'm going to go meet up with Sam, but you can go ahead, Emily."

Emily opened her mouth to tell Nicole that she had

other plans, but then she remembered her grandmother's encouragement. Trying to forgive and forget was the first step. So was hanging out with Nicole the next one?

Nicole reached out her hand. Emily grasped it and allowed Nicole to pull her to her feet.

"You like the Scrambler, don't you?" Lily put her hand on Emily's arm. "I love that ride, but it makes Nicole sick. Last year she puked all over my hair. It was totally gross."

"Yeah, I like the Scrambler." As Emily said the words she felt guilty for not taking her cousins on it yesterday. But that was then, and Emily pushed those thoughts out of her mind, realizing there was nothing she could do about it now.

"Cool. Then will you at least go on that one with me? I don't want to go on it alone." Lily grinned, brushing her reddish-brown hair back from her face.

"Okay, I suppose."

It's just a few rides. Maybe Nicole and her friends will even learn to like me. It might help things.

Emily walked along with the cheerleaders, and she had to admit she liked the feeling of being with the popular crowd.

Besides, she hadn't promised anything with the sleepover. Maybe it would work, maybe not. But she wasn't going to worry about that now. She only had one thing on her mind . . . the Scrambler.

THEY RODE RIDES most of the afternoon. After going on the Squirrel Cages three times in a row and asking the carnival worker to spin them each time, Emily was starting to feel sick. From the look on Lily's face, she was too.

"Okay, I think I'm done." Lily wrapped her arms around her stomach.

"Yeah, me too. I can only be spun, squished, and jerked around so much."

"Well, I suppose we could head over to the mutton busting; that's always fun." Kaitlin tucked her green shirt back into her jean shorts.

"The what?" Nicole laughed. Since she got sick on rides, Nicole hadn't ridden on any of them, and she still looked perfect. Instead, she'd followed them around, holding their sunglasses and sodas. "Mutton busting sounds like an English casserole gone bad."

"You haven't seen it?" Kaitlin asked.

"No, I mostly stick to talking to guys and eating the food." Nicole tucked her thumbs into her jean shorts.

"I, uh, haven't seen it either." Emily twirled a strand of hair around her finger.

"Oh, it's so cute. Little kids under seven sign up to ride a sheep. Their parents put bike helmets on them and then an adult lifts them onto the sheep." Kaitlin chuckled to herself. "The kid holds on for dear life. It's the funniest thing ever, and they win a pair of Justin boots for staying on the longest."

"It sounds sort of cool." Emily glanced at the faces of the other girls, gauging their response.

"Actually, I'd rather just head out to Emily's house. You know, to see what's going on out there," Nicole said.

"Well, I should talk to my grandma first to make sure it's okay," Emily said.

"Why wouldn't it be okay?" Nicole cocked an eyebrow.

"Well, because there's a lot going on—with the fair and

all the video people at our house. I don't think Grandma would be very happy if I showed up with a lot of extra guests without asking. But if you wait a minute I can run over and ask Grandma at the fair office. It's right over there." Emily pointed.

"Sure, whatever, go ask." Nicole forced her lips into a tight smile.

Emily could tell Nicole was trying to be nice, trying to hold her tongue. Each time Nicole opened her mouth Emily waited for the hurtful remark, but none came. *Maybe this is a turning point*, she thought.

She also had to admit she'd had fun going on rides and stuff. Maybe Grandma was right; maybe people could move past old conflicts if given the chance.

Emily hurried toward the fair office and slipped in the side door.

"Hi, Mrs. Carter." Emily waved to her grandmother's friend.

"Oh hi, Emily. What are you up to?"

"Well, I just wanted to run in and ask my grandma a quick question." She walked across the room to the closed door. "Do you think it's okay?" She placed her hand on the doorknob.

"Well, your grandma went home. She told me to tell you she tried to call your cell phone. She said you'll be riding home with your grandpa later."

Emily took her phone from her back pocket and, sure enough, there were four missed calls from her grandmother. She tried to call her grandma back but there was no answer.

"Is Grandpa in there?" Emily pointed to the back room,

where she could hear voices. "Do you think it's okay if I talk to him for a minute?"

"Well, I'm sure your grandpa wouldn't mind, but things are pretty heated in there. I can't hear what they're saying exactly, but I can for sure hear that there are some unhappy campers."

Emily scrunched her nose. "Yeah, well, I don't want to get in the middle of that. Do you think it would be okay if I left a note for Grandpa?"

"Sure, I'll make sure I give it to him when he gets out." Hannah handed Emily a piece of paper and a pen.

"Great, and I'll have my cell phone if he needs to call me."

"Are you going to be somewhere around the fair-grounds? Maybe over at the grandstand for the big event?"

"Actually, I'm gonna head home. I've been hanging out around here a lot lately . . ." She let her voice trail off as she figured out what to write:

Dear Grandpa, I got a ride home with Kaitlin, who is a friend of Nicole Evans. See you at home later. Emily

Emily gave the note to Hannah, who promised to pass it on. When she walked out she noticed that Sam, Arielle, Natalie, and Jordan were waiting.

"Hey, there you are. The pig wrestling starts in thirty minutes. Are you going to join us and cheer on the guys?" Arielle asked her.

"Oh yeah, pig wrestling. Is that today?"

"Yeah. Duh, we talked about it yesterday." Sam softly

slugged her shoulder. "After that we're heading over to the grandstand."

Kaitlin jingled her car keys in front of Emily's face to distract her.

"Uh, actually, I'm going back to the farm. We're going to be having a sleepover."

"A sleepover, huh?" Sam scoffed, staring pointedly at Nicole. "How convenient. Come on, guys."

Sam signaled to the others, and Emily felt her heart fall. *Am I doing the right thing? Making the right choice?*

Deep down, Emily knew she wasn't, but she was in too deep. There was no way to back out now.

Chapter Eighteen

S am trudged toward the small arena where the pig wrestling would soon be held. Exiting the auditorium next to the arena, a line of 4-H members trailed out. Disappointment filled the faces of the kids who hadn't won.

When Sam and his friends got to the arena, they saw cowboys sitting on top of the corral's metal fence. They matched, sort of, with their jeans, boots, colorful shirts, and brown cowboy hats. Jordan, of course, had to take a picture.

When Sam saw the stands were packed, his stomach turned. The heat beat down on his head, and he felt like he was going to be sick.

"You ready for this?" Sam asked Jordan.

"Are you kidding? We're going to get that pig and win. We'll show these cowboys what city boys can do!"

Sam smiled, but he didn't feel quite so confident. He'd imagined it would be a small event held behind one of the animal barns, nothing like this.

Tall bleachers circled the small ring, which was filled with two feet of mud. Some of Arielle's friends waved to them from one of the bleacher rows, and as they climbed up the steps, everyone squeezed together to make room for them to sit. Before the pig was released into the ring, it too was also slathered with the icky mud.

Arielle pulled her canvas bag off her shoulder. "Guess what?"

Sam looked her direction, attempting a smile. "What?"

"Natalie and I made some T-shirts for you with your names." She pulled four gray T-shirts out of the bag and tossed one to each of the guys.

Sam held his up. On the front was a drawing of a pig sitting in a barrel. He couldn't help but smile. "Gee, thanks."

"Yeah, turn it around and look at the back," Natalie urged.

Sam turned it around and saw his name.

"Thanks."

"Sure thing. Go ahead and put it on."

Sam slipped it over the T-shirt he was already wearing. He'd purposefully worn his least-favorite pair of jeans and old tennis shoes, knowing they were going to end up a mess.

As soon as everyone had their shirts on, Arielle had them stand so she could take their picture. Sam was glad everyone was excited, but he would have been just as happy to quit and walk away from this particular competition. As he sat in the bleachers, shoulder to shoulder between Jake and Jordan, Sam wondered again why he'd let them talk him into this.

The event started with groups of little kids chasing piglets. Everyone cheered each time the kids got their hands on the pig. They cheered even louder when the kids slipped in the mud during their chase. Only one group actually got the pig into the barrel.

The men's division was next, and the first guys who entered the pig-wrestling ring made it look anything but easy. The goal of the contest was to catch a pig as a group of four, pick it up, and dump it into a barrel in the middle of the ring.

The first group of guys managed to catch the pig, but the buzzer went off right before they got it into the barrel. The second group of guys didn't even get a firm grip on the pig. They tried to race up to it and ended up flat on their faces in the mud more than once.

Paul leaned across Jake. "We're up after these guys. They look old and fat. I'm sure it will take them the whole time just to cross the pen."

Paul chuckled. "Oink, oink."

"I'm not too sure," Jake shook his head. "These are last year's winners. They've been farmers twice as long as you've been alive. If anyone knows how to tame a pig, it's them."

"Yeah," Jordan mumbled. "I've heard about these guys. I think I saw them on TV. They call themselves the Pig Whisperers." He laughed, and Paul and Jake joined him.

"Really?" Natalie turned to them, eyes wide.

Jordan laughed harder. "No, it was just a joke."

Sam wasn't in the mood for joking around. Instead, he kept his eyes on the timekeeper guy with the orange flag. When the flag dropped, he expected the men to rush forward like the others had done. Instead, they waited and then slowly began their trek across the pen. They didn't move too fast. They didn't make a noise. In fact, it seemed as if the whole crowd was holding its breath in anticipation.

"Look at that. The pig isn't running. He doesn't even realize they're coming." Jake pointed.

Sam felt his shoulders tighten with anxiety. *Were they going to do it?* Then he watched in amazement as the men circled the pig, picked him up, and deposited him in the bucket as easily as if they were throwing a Styrofoam cup into the trash.

"That's the way we have to do it." Sam stood, knowing they were next. He looked at the clock keeper, waiting to hear the time.

"Twenty-nine point five seconds!" the man yelled out.

"No way," Jake mumbled. "We can never beat that."

"Hey, stop jinxing us." Paul socked his shoulder playfully. "We know the plan, right? We're going to do it just like that—maybe a little faster."

"Next up," the man on the microphone called, "are the Baconators! They are about to fry that pig, right boys?"

"That's right!" Sam heard himself saying.

"Yippee!" Jordan called beside him.

They entered the gate, and Sam was surprised by how thick the mud was. It wasn't like the soft clay at the soft bottom in Heather Creek. Instead, it had a thicker consistency—like cement that had partially set.

They had to place their hands on the rail near the gate and watch as the pig was released. The pig was huge—bigger than the others had been.

"What is that? Godzilla pig?" he heard Jordan mutter.

The blaring of a horn told them to start, and he knew the seconds were ticking by. Sam forgot about getting the best time. He focused on the pig and just hoped they'd get it into the barrel.

He began inching closer, noticing the others doing the same. Jordan moved faster than the others, and Sam picked up his pace to catch up. The mud was slippery. It was like walking on ice, or grease. With each step he had to pause slightly to balance himself.

"Come on, guys. You're moving too slow. Pick up the pace." The words were barely out of Jordan's mouth when his feet slipped out from under him. Sam didn't know someone could fall that fast. Jordan landed on his back with his arms and legs sprawled everywhere. Seeing this, the pig squealed and bolted in Sam's direction.

"Catch him!" Jake yelled, scurrying after the pig.

Sam set his feet, scrunched down, and prepared to catch the pig. It approached, and he dove for it. His arms stretched out and wrapped around the pig, but it was just like trying to catch a large, slippery bullet. His hands felt the bristly hairs of the pig briefly, and then it was gone. Even though the pig moved on, Sam's body continued falling forward. He tried to catch himself, but it was useless. His hands, arms, and chest hit the mud first and then his face.

"Get up!" Sam heard Paul yell. "Get up! Get up!"

Sam struggled to his feet, but the ground was too slippery. Just as he started to rise, his feet slid again, and his body splashed back into the mud.

Sam tried a third time, and this time he made it up. He tried to wipe the mud from his eyes, but it did little good. He half-opened them and mostly listened for the shouts of his friends.

"We got it. We got it." He heard Jordan call.

Sam reached them and the pig, and tried to help them hoist it up. It was no use. The pig wriggled and squealed, sounding like it was being butchered. Sam wrapped his arms around it just as the buzzer went off.

"No way," Paul muttered.

The crowd laughed and cheered—mostly laughed—and Sam felt heat rising to his cheeks. They'd just made fools of themselves in front of everyone they knew.

"Good try." He felt Jordan's hand on his back.

"Maybe next year." Jake wrapped his arm around Sam's shoulders as they exited the arena.

"Or maybe not," Sam mumbled, happy to get his feet on firm ground again. He'd barely made it two steps out of the ring when he felt Arielle's arms around him.

"That was amazing!" She placed a quick kiss on his muddy cheek and giggled. "Watching that was the best thing ever. I'm so proud of you."

"Really?" Sam straightened his shoulders.

"Come on." Arielle tugged on his arms. "There are some hoses over here. They use them to wash off the cows and pigs."

"Are you calling me a pig?"

Arielle reached up and pulled a clump of mud from Sam's hair, flicking it to the ground. "Yes. Yes, I am."

Chapter Nineteen

The evening air was still thick and muggy, and Charlotte looked forward to the days ahead when cool breezes arrived with the dinner bell. Most of the video crew had left for the evening, and now only a few of the guys sat around the dining room table working on the storyboard for the video.

She opened the window wider, hoping for fresh air . . . and hoping to see Bob sauntering in from the barn. No such luck on either.

"More coffee?" Charlotte asked Will and Buck. Both men had been especially nice to her after she'd returned home. Perhaps they were making up for the fiasco with the horse earlier in the week.

"If it's not too much trouble." Buck held up his mug and forced a smile.

"Oh, not at all." Charlotte poured another cup and filled a plate with walnut-cherry cookies, placing it on the table in front of them.

She'd checked in with Bob, and he seemed to be taking things in stride.

"These cookies are amazing!" Will exclaimed, eating a cookie with one bite.

"Glad you like them," Charlotte said.

The sound of a car rumbling down the driveway caused Charlotte to look out the window. She expected to see Pete's truck, doubting Sam would leave the fair this early. Instead, it was a car Charlotte didn't recognize.

She watched as it parked and four teen girls piled out. As they got closer, Charlotte saw that it was Emily, Nicole, Lily, and another girl she recognized from the school.

Charlotte waved, and Emily waved back. She was partially pleased that Emily had obviously made amends after yesterday's disagreement with Nicole, but her smile turned into a frown when she noticed the girls grabbing sleeping bags, pillows, and overnight bags from the trunk of the car.

Emily hurried ahead, and Charlotte met her on the front porch.

"Hey, Grandma." She looked up at Charlotte expectantly.

"I see you brought some friends."

"Yeah, I was going to ask you about that. Can they stay the night?" Emily shoved her hands into the front pockets of her jean shorts and swayed from side to side.

"Were you asking, or telling?" Charlotte tapped her chin with one finger.

"Ummm, well, they just sort of invited themselves, and I didn't know what to say."

"Do you think Shae Lynne coming tomorrow has anything to do with this?"

Emily nodded, and Charlotte could see the anxiety in her granddaughter's face. It would be hard on her and Bob having three more teens in the house, but she knew it would be even harder on Emily if the girls weren't allowed to spend the night.

Charlotte saw the girls nearing, and she stepped closer and lowered her voice. "They can stay tonight, but from now on you need to ask permission first. Also, you can't hang around and bother Shae Lynne when she arrives. Let her approach you first."

Emily nodded. "Understood." Then she turned to her friends.

"Well, this is the farm. Nothing special."

"Can we look around?" Nicole's eyes focused on the camera and light stands that were scattered around the farm. "I promise we won't touch a thing."

"Maybe later." Charlotte motioned to the house. "Have you all gotten permission to spend the night here?" she asked.

The girls nodded in unison.

"Ok, then let's get your things inside and I'll introduce you to the video producers."

Nicole's eyes widened in a way that made Charlotte partly glad she was able to give this to Emily—a chance to show Nicole up for one day. A chance to be the talk of the town.

Is that okay, Lord? Charlotte wondered as she held the door open for the girls. *Is it wrong to want my granddaughter to have something to talk about? To feel special about?*

Charlotte stood back and watched as the producers introduced themselves to Emily's friends. The girls gushed over the prospect of seeing Shae Lynne and ignored Emily when she offered to show them her room.

Charlotte sighed. *They are here for only one thing, and it's not Emily.*

All of Charlotte's attempts to let the week's events run off her failed as she approached the table. "Girls, why don't you take your things up to Emily's room. Then I can make you a snack if you're hungry."

"Do we have to?" Nicole asked, looking at Charlotte doe-eyed and not wanting to leave the video planners. Then, seeing the answer in Charlotte's gaze, she turned to Emily. "So, where's your room? I'm sure it's just great."

Charlotte could hear the sarcasm in Nicole's tone, and she almost regretted telling Emily to try to befriend the girl. Then again, doing the right thing was the right thing, even if it meant holding your tongue and giving yourself time to stew.

SAM SHIVERED AS HE TURNED into the driveway. The night was warm, but his clothes were still wet from getting hosed off, causing a chill to race down his spine.

Eighties music was playing on the radio, and Jordan shook his head and turned it down.

"What is this stuff?" Jordan whined. "I thought that music disappeared ages ago, along with parachute pants and spiked hair."

"It's either that or country." Sam changed the station. "I can't always get the rock station."

Sam thought about all the CDs and DVDs he could have bought with the prize money—if they'd won. If the pig hadn't been so quick. If they'd done a better job at figuring out their strategy.

"Do you have Internet?" Jordan asked, almost bouncing in his seat. "Natalie said she was going to post the video of our pig wrestling on YouTube. I want to e-mail the link to all our friends back home."

"Internet . . . well, our connection is slow. We still have dial-up, if you can believe it." Sam chuckled. "And besides, I wouldn't call that pig wrestling, if I were you. More like taking a mud bath."

Sam twirled his finger in his ear. "I think I'm going to be finding mud in unexpected places for a month."

"Whatever. I can't wait to see our mud-bath photos. I want to put them all over MySpace."

"Are you kidding? But we didn't even win."

"No one has to know that, although if they actually watch the video I believe they'll figure that out."

Sam parked the car, and they were getting out just in time to see Will and Buck exiting the house.

All of the crew and cameras were gone, but Sam could see that some of the stands for lights were still in position—waiting for tomorrow. Waiting for Shae Lynne to show up.

"See you guys tomorrow?" Will waved in their direction.

"We'll be here, sir." Sam answered.

"You and the rest of Bedford High." Will laughed but Buck didn't seem quite as amused. Sam followed his gaze to the upstairs window of Emily's room, where three girls' faces, none of them Emily's, peered down.

"Dude, you don't have it so bad." Jordan shook his head as they headed toward the house. "The best food. Your own car. Cute girls."

"Think so, huh?" Sam asked. "Awesome, that means you can help me with chores again tomorrow."

AFTER PUSHING HER BED against the wall, Emily had just enough room to line up four sleeping bags on the floor. Emily hugged her pillow to her chest and sat quietly as she listened to the other girls talking about the fair—about the cute guys they met at the cheerleaders' booth and about going clothes shopping next week in Harding. They neither invited her into the conversation nor invited her shopping with them. Emily tried not to let her anger show, especially when they burst into laughter talking about the "losers" in the pig wrestling. Didn't they know that Sam was one of those guys, and he was far from a loser?

A knock sounded at the door, and Emily guessed it was her grandma coming to tell them to quiet down.

"Come in," she called.

The door swung open, and Emily was surprised to see Ashley standing there. As soon as she saw her friend—and the hurt expression on Ashley's face—it all came back. They were supposed to go see Hunter's barrel race *and Ashley was supposed to spend the night!*

Emily's heart skipped a beat, and she jumped to her feet. "Ashley!" A heaviness filled the pit of her stomach.

"I thought we had plans. Did you forget?"

Laughter burst from the other girls, and Emily didn't know what they were laughing at. Maybe it was the cowboy hat Ashley wore. Or the bandanna tied around her neck. Or maybe it was just because they thrived on making everyone else feel bad. Ashley opened her mouth and then closed it again. Then she turned and hurried down the stairs.

Emily vaulted over the other girls. "Ashley, wait!"

"Oh, no. It looks like someone has her feelings hurt. Maybe she feels—"

Emily didn't wait around for Nicole to finish. She hurried down the stairs just in time to see Ashley rushing out the kitchen door.

"Ashley, wait!"

Ashley turned, and in the moonlight Emily could make out her red, watery eyes. In the driveway her grandma was talking to Mrs. Givens. Emily grabbed Ashley's arm, and Ashley paused.

"I can't believe you did this! You skipped the barrel races to hang out with them? Hunter is going to be so hurt. He won, you know. And he asked where you were. I, of course, had no idea."

Emily knew that even though Ashley didn't mention herself, she was also hurt.

"I don't know what happened. I just totally forgot. The day, it just got away from me. Everything was crazy," she said.

"Yeah, I suppose. Or you found a better option. You have your famous singer visiting tomorrow, and your popular friends tonight." Ashley shrugged. "What do you need me for?"

Melody started to back out the car, waving good-bye to them, and Ashley motioned for her to stop.

Looking confused, Melody rolled down the window. "You aren't staying?"

"No." Ashley shook her head.

"You're not staying?" Emily echoed.

"Why would I stay? You made other plans."

"But I didn't mean to make other plans. I didn't mean for everything to happen like this. I feel horrible. I've been telling Hunter I'd be there . . . and you." A lump formed in Emily's throat. "I'd rather be with you than with them." Emily nodded her head toward her bedroom window.

"Yeah, well, I really don't want to stay. I don't want to be here. I'm not mad." Ashley shrugged. "Not totally. I just need to go home now."

Emily's shoulders sank as she watched Ashley trudge back to her mom's car with her overnight bag in hand. Neither Ashley nor her mom waved as they drove away.

Grandma approached, and Emily couldn't look into her eyes. Instead she focused on the peeling paint of the porch steps.

"So it seems that things didn't turn out today quite like they were supposed to."

Emily shook her head. "No, not at all."

Charlotte let out a heavy sigh. "Yeah, but the truth is that you have three girls you need to entertain for the night. And . . . tomorrow is another busy day."

"Grandma? Can I sleep with Trudy tonight?"

"In the barn?" Her grandma wrapped an arm around her shoulder. "I don't think so."

"Yeah, well, I think I'd be more comfortable. I don't like this at all."

"Live and learn, Emily. That's what all of us do every day. Live and learn."

Chapter
Twenty

Charlotte awoke Thursday to the sound of a horse whinnying just outside the window. She peered out to see a muscular man in a leather vest and no shirt riding into the pasture.

"Oh my!" She pulled on her bathrobe over her nightgown.

"What is it?" Bob sat up, rubbed his eyes, and glanced at the clock radio with surprise. "Is it really after seven o'clock?"

"Yes, it is. And a young Arnold Schwarzenegger is riding a body double of Britney. I guess they gave up on trying to ride her."

Bob rose and hurried to the bathroom. "I can't believe I slept in," he called. "I have to get going on the morning chores before they start filming."

"Don't worry. I'm sure Pete took care of that. Besides, I don't blame you for sleeping in. Those kids were up all night. I even heard Christopher's voice among the bunch. I think they were all wound up with the idea of Shae Lynne showing up today."

"Yes, well, maybe that means they'll sleep in a while. I don't want those kids pouncing on her as soon as she comes."

Charlotte dressed and then ran a comb through her hair. "So, did they tell you what time she'd be here?"

"Nope. I never heard, but I imagine when she comes rolling up in that big bus of hers we'll all know it."

"Yup." Charlotte slipped on her shoes. "I imagine it will be quite a show."

"Oatmeal for breakfast?" Charlotte moved toward the bedroom door.

"How about oatmeal *and* sausage?" Bob peeked around the corner of the bathroom and grinned.

Charlotte chuckled. "Well, this is a special day. I'll call you when it's ready."

Charlotte noticed the house was completely quiet as she hurried to the kitchen to get some coffee on. Outside was a different story. Cameras were already set up near the barn. The door to the wardrobe trailer was open, and Charlotte saw Tami and Tracy hurrying in that direction.

Charlotte took some coffee cake out of the fridge and sliced it. Then she started a fresh pot of coffee. She paused as she walked past the kitchen window, startled by the young woman sitting on the porch. Toby was sitting by her, or rather, on her.

"That dog," Charlotte mumbled to herself. She hurried out the side door, noting that the warmth of the morning promised it would be another hot day. She hurried with quick steps toward where the young woman sat.

"Toby, you're such a bother."

The girl glanced up, apparently surprised by Charlotte's quick approach.

Toby slumped back with an "I've been caught" look on her face.

"Oh, he's okay." The young woman patted Toby's head. "I called him to me." The woman was thin and petite. She had long blonde hair that was pulled back in an easy ponytail. She wore no makeup on her face, but she had a natural, simple beauty.

"Are you sure?" Charlotte set her hands on her hips. "Toby's a she, and she has a way of butting into other people's business."

"No, really, it's okay. I love dogs—especially farm dogs—but I'm on the road so much that I decided it wouldn't be fair to have one at home."

"Oh, so do you travel with this group often?"

The young woman's eyes lifted in surprise. "Uh, yeah, I suppose you can say that."

"Well, if you're on the road that much I bet you'd enjoy a nice cup of coffee and some homemade coffee cake. Would you like to come in and join me?"

"Sure." She stood, and a large smile filled her face. "I'm Shayla, by the way."

"Nice to meet you Shayla." Charlotte stretched out her hand. "And I'm Charlotte."

The young woman followed Charlotte into the house. Charlotte opened the screen door for her.

Shayla paused in the doorway. "Oh, my goodness. I love your home."

Charlotte glanced around at the worn wood floor. The dingy, butter-yellow cupboards were at least fifty years old. She noticed all the junk—Christopher's cross, her old teacup, and a hundred other things she'd stored in every nook and cranny. She sighed as she realized the living room was still a mess from where they moved the furniture. "Well, it's really nothing special . . ." Charlotte let her voice trail off.

Shayla stepped inside. "No. It is special. It's so cozy and warm. Inviting. To me, it says *home*."

"Well, to my husband, Bob, it says *cluttered*, but I'm not very good at getting rid of stuff. I've kept some of my mom's things and some things that belonged to Bob's mom."

Shayla sighed contently and moved to Charlotte's hutch. "I love your dishes. My grandma used to have the apple-patterned ones just like that. Oh, and you have Depression glass. When I have a free day on the road I like to go junking, and sometimes I come up lucky."

"Junking?" Charlotte chuckled. "Yes, my husband does sometimes call my stuff junk."

Shayla turned and placed a hand over her heart. "No, I'm so sorry. I didn't mean it like that. It's just my word for antiquing. It's my favorite thing to do. In fact, I'd love a kitchen just like this someday."

She picked up a small bird figurine that Charlotte had owned since she was a little girl and turned it over in her hands.

"Yes, well some people have to hunt for their antiques, and I suppose I just keep my stuff until it's old." Charlotte chuckled. "And personally, I've talked to Bob a few times about remodeling the kitchen, but there's always something that comes up."

Charlotte's mind turned to the kids. Ever since they'd come to Heather Creek Farm they'd taken up all her time—especially that extra time she'd devoted to her hobbies.

"Speaking of old, we'd better get some coffee while it's fresh. Do you use cream or sugar?"

Shayla smiled. "Yes, both please. I'm a wimp. I can't handle the black stuff." She washed her hands in the sink and then helped herself to a piece of coffee cake on the counter. She had a natural way about the kitchen, a way that made Charlotte like her instantly. She wasn't one of those uppity Nashville types that Charlotte expected to see later that day.

Charlotte poured two cups of coffee and then took them to the table.

"This is the best coffee cake ever," Shayla said. "Seriously, I could just take you on the road with me. Of course, I'm sure your family would hunt you down." A warm smile filled Shayla's face, and Charlotte thought she recognized that smile.

"Yes, I'm sure they would, and to be truthful, I'm not sure I'd do so well on the road anyway, although I'm sure my granddaughter Emily would think it was very glamorous."

"Glamorous is what it's not. I mean, I love it and all, but I really only have an hour in the morning for myself. Most days are usually filled with meetings, lunches, or charity events. And by four we're already doing a sound check at the venue. After that it's a quick dinner and then a meet and . . ."

Shayla glanced up. "You know, just meetings with fans and stuff. Pretty soon it's showtime, and then the rest is repeated the next day."

Charlotte didn't know what part of the show this young woman helped with, but she sure seemed comfortable in her own skin. And then as Charlotte sat with her she began to wonder. *Could this Shayla be Shae Lynne?* Maybe it was a stage name.

No, don't be silly. This girl is much too innocent and sweet to be that famous singer everyone's talking about.

"Look at me, I've just been jabbering away. Enough about me," Shayla said. "Tell me about you."

So Charlotte did. She told the girl about the farm and about the kids. She told her about some of the challenges of the year and yet some of the ways God had blessed them too. Charlotte also mentioned that more than anything she wished she could have another day with her daughter to tell Denise how much she loved her and to walk through the sunflowers once again, like they used to when Denise was young.

Tears filled the young girl's eyes, and she dabbed the corners with her napkin.

"I'm sorry. I didn't mean to make you sad." Charlotte got up and poured them both another cup of coffee. "It's been hard, and we miss Denise and all, but Bob and Pete and I really do enjoy having the kids here. And we all enjoy each other."

"Oh, it's not only the story that's sad," the girl sniffled. "It's . . . well, what I'm trying to say is that things have just been really hard for me lately. So many people tell me I should be honored to do what I do, and I am, but there's a part of me that wouldn't mind having a cabin in the woods somewhere with a husband and a few dogs. To lead a simple life. To not wake up in a new town and have to look at our schedule to figure out where I am. I'd love to have a family and a house like this, filled with love."

More tears came, and Shayla covered her face with her hands. She made no sound, but her shoulders shook slightly. Charlotte didn't try to give her pat answers. She didn't trying to overstep her bounds. Instead, she put a hand on the girl's shoulder and silently prayed for her.

Streams of light filtered through the windows, and as the room brightened Charlotte began to see everything more clearly. She had a feeling, deep down, that their farm hadn't been chosen by accident. She knew that God had brought this crew—as crazy as it was—not just to help with some of the financial burdens. Perhaps he'd also brought these people here for their sake, too.

Life on the Stevensons' farm was simple, but their love for each other and for God was evident. And maybe those who visited would walk away from the farm a little different— more settled—than before.

After a few minutes, Charlotte stood, remembering she still needed to make Bob's breakfast. She also had an unexplained urge to do something for all those who were on the farm. "You know, I can make some more coffee cake for the rest of the crew. Do you think they would enjoy that?"

"Are you kidding? I bet they'd really like that." Shayla smiled, but Charlotte could tell her eyes were a little bit puffy.

"And what about Shae Lynne? Do you think she'd like coffee cake?"

The young woman laughed and a smile filled her face. It was a smile Charlotte recognized . . . from the posters hanging around the fair.

"Yeah." The young woman stood and followed Charlotte into the kitchen. "Since she's already eaten two pieces I imagine she would."

Chapter
Twenty-One

By the time the teens woke up the production crew was in full swing. Charlotte didn't tell the kids she'd already spent the morning talking with Shae Lynne. She just enjoyed the surprised looks on her grandchildren's faces when Shae Lynne approached her and offered a big hug.

"Charlotte, please would you introduce me to everyone?"

Charlotte introduced her grandchildren first and then Jordan. Finally, she introduced Nicole, Lily, and Kaitlin, who looked as if they were going to burst with excitement.

"Can I get my photo taken with you?" Nicole nearly squealed the question.

Shae Lynne chuckled. "Sure, why don't I get one with each of you?" She glanced at the boys. "Then you can have something fun to post on MySpace."

Jordan's jaw dropped open as if he wondered how she knew that's exactly what he planned on doing.

Shae Lynne posed with each of the teens, and Charlotte had to admit that if it weren't for the wide smile she would have a hard time believing it was the same girl she'd talked to that morning. Shae Lynne must have added extensions to her hair because it seemed to have grown six inches in the last two hours. Not only that, it was teased up and sprayed. It had sort of a wind-blown look, but the wind wasn't blowing. More than that, it didn't move an inch as she smiled and posed.

Her makeup was thick and rather dark, and Charlotte guessed that it was done that way for the cameras. She wore skinny jeans and a white, flowing blouse.

When the photos were done, Shae Lynne clapped her hands together. "Y'all are welcome to stay and watch, but you have to be as quiet as possible. Most videos use sound-tracks recorded in studio, but I like to actually sing when we film. It prevents me from looking like I'm lip-synching." A laugh split the air, and Charlotte looked behind her to note Pete approaching.

He pushed his John Deere cap back from his forehead and smiled. "No lip-synching, huh? Now, that's refresh-ing." Pete stretched out his hand. "I'm Pete by the way."

Shae Lynne's eyes brightened. "Pete. It's wonderful to meet you. I'm Shae Lynne."

He shrugged. "Yeah, I know. My girlfriend has one of your CDs."

"Really? Wow, I'm honored."

Charlotte took a step back, noting the interaction. If she didn't know better, she'd think that Shae Lynne was actu-ally blushing.

Shae Lynne looked down at her outfit. She placed a hand on her hair. "Oh, sorry for my getup. You know how the video thing works."

"Actually I don't. This is the first time I've ever experi-enced anything like this."

"Really?" Shae Lynne cocked her head. "I thought you were the actor to play . . ." She paused. "To play my *love* interest in the video," she cooed, smiling.

Snickers came from Sam and Jordan, and Charlotte immediately turned and narrowed her gaze at them.

Pete laughed. "Now *that's* funny. No, I'm just Farmer Pete." He spread his arm. "And this is my place. Or rather it's my parents' place, and I help out around here."

Shae Lynne touched her neck, and Charlotte could clearly see the red creeping up to her face.

A horse that looked similar to Britney rounded the corner; the hunky-looking man with the vest was still riding her.

Charlotte pointed. "That's probably your leading man."

Shae Lynne's nose scrunched in disapproval. "Please tell me that's not so."

Charlotte shrugged.

"Shae, do you have a minute?" Will was carrying a clipboard in his hands. "I wanted to go over the shot list with you before we get started."

"Sure, and there's, uh, something I wanted to talk about with you too," she said, striding off.

"Wow, Uncle Pete. Shae Lynne thought you were going to be the main guy in her video, not just the dude driving the tractor." Emily seemed impressed.

He shrugged. "That's only because she had all that goopy makeup on her eyes and wasn't able to see clearly."

"Uncle Pete." Emily slugged his arm. "I think she's beautiful."

Charlotte hung out with the kids for the rest of the morning. They watched as Shae Lynne sang in front of the barn. And during her break they watched as the crew shot more video inside the barn.

They spent at least an hour shooting the stalls and hay loft from various angles. They even made Trudy a star by filming her.

"Is our cow going to be in the video?" Christopher walked over and scratched behind Trudy's ear.

"Yeah, she most likely will be. We're taping all this as background. Then if we need to green-screen it later we can go back and do that."

"Green-screen it?"

"Shae Lynne likes to feature her band in her videos. As you can see, they're not here, and they won't be here until they fly in to do the concert on Saturday night. So we videotape the barn and then we videotape the band against a green screen and splice them together."

"Wow, I wonder what Trudy will think about that."

"Do you think she'll know?" Nicole frowned. "Honestly, she's a cow. Don't be so dumb."

"Nicole." Charlotte tried to keep her voice calm. "We don't talk to each other that way."

"Uh . . ." Nicole got a sheepish look on her face. "I'm sorry. I didn't mean it."

"I know. I think we're all getting a little tired and cranky around here. It was a long night of anticipation and a lot has been going on around the farm this morning. It might be best if you and your friends head home. We'll just let the video crew finish up what they're working on."

Nicole frowned and opened her mouth. Charlotte was

wondering what was going to come out, but instead of arguing Nicole turned and headed toward the house.

"Who cares? I got my photo with Shae Lynne, which means I won fifty bucks," Charlotte heard her saying.

"Are the girls leaving?" Shae Lynne strolled into the barn.

"Actually, they are. They slept over last night, and now that they've seen you, they're ready to head back to the fair."

Shae Lynne nodded, but Charlotte could tell she wasn't listening.

"Uh, do you know where Pete is?" Shae Lynne asked.

"I think I saw him behind the barn changing the oil in the tractor."

Shae Lynne turned to leave the barn, and Charlotte's gaze moved from Emily to Sam. "What do you think that was about?"

Sam shrugged. "I don't know, but I want to find out." He nodded to Jordan, and the two boys sauntered outside as if they weren't following.

EMILY JOGGED UP THE STAIRS to see if Nicole, Lily, and Kaitlin needed any help loading their things into Kaitlin's car. Emily had tried to enjoy the morning with them the best she could, but the only thing on her mind was calling up Ashley and Hunter and trying to fix things.

"Oh, my gosh!" Kaitlin's voice caused Emily to pause at the top of the steps, right in front of her bedroom door.

"What?" Nicole sounded upset, most likely because she'd been asked to head home.

"Look at Emily's closet. I've never seen such a sad bunch of clothes in my life. Is this honestly all she owns?"

"Yeah, well, what do you expect, living with her grandparents, being totally poor, having no fashion sense." It was Lily talking. "I mean she's so skinny and plain. If you ask me, I feel totally sorry for her. I mean, she's never going to get a boyfriend. Never going to—"

"Emily?"

Emily had been so focused on the conversation in the room that she hadn't heard Christopher approaching.

"What?" she snapped, turning to him.

He took a step back. "Man, I was just going to ask you if you wanted your CDs signed by Shae Lynne. She said she'd sign them for us."

"Not now," Emily hissed. She turned toward the door, and then to Christopher again, unsure of what to do, what to say.

The door swung open, and three faces stared at her with looks of half-pity and half-annoyance. She could tell that they knew she'd heard every word.

"Hey, Emily." Nicole swung her backpack over her shoulder. "I think I got everything, but if I left any clothes or whatever, you can just keep them."

Nicole smiled, and Lily snickered. Emily didn't even want to see Kaitlin's reaction. But with Christopher blocking the stairway, Emily turned and ran into the one place she could go to be alone. She darted into the bathroom and slammed the door, leaning her back against it and sliding to the floor.

Suddenly nothing good that had happened that week mattered. Her ribbons didn't count. The fact that she had one of her favorite singers at her house didn't matter. All Emily knew was that her heart hurt. Bad. And that she'd messed up, big time. She had totally ruined things with the friends she did have while trying to befriend the girls who lived to make her life miserable.

Emily pulled her knees to her chest and rested her forehead on her knees. Her lower lip trembled, and she wished she could cry. Wished she could release the pain. Instead she just sat there and wanted everything to be different.

OVER THE NEXT FEW HOURS, Charlotte learned that the video crew taped hard, fast, and continuously. She enjoyed watching the process, as did the kids. Sam and Jordan liked talking with Shae Lynne during the breaks, and Christopher had a hundred and one questions about how the cameras and other machines worked. The best part was that other than a few more cars driving down their country road, it seemed like the attention given to the video shoot had died down.

Reluctantly, Charlotte glanced at her watch after lunch, realizing she had to get to the fair for her shift at the Amen Pies booth. She had headed inside for her purse when she noticed Emily sitting by herself on the couch. It was only then Charlotte realized she hadn't seen Emily outside all day.

"Emily?" Charlotte approached, sitting beside her. "Is everything okay?"

Emily shrugged but didn't comment.

Charlotte patted her granddaughter's hand. "Are you feeling bad about Ashley and Hunter?"

Emily nodded, her lips pressed into a thin line.

"And did something else happen with Nicole? More than her winning that bet, which really made me mad, just so you know."

Emily nodded again.

"Well, maybe tonight, after I get home, we can talk about it." Charlotte rose, glancing at her watch again. She knew if she didn't leave now she'd be late.

"Grandma, no. Wait." Emily grabbed her arm. "I need you to help me. I need you to fix things. Can you call Mrs. Givens for me? She likes you. Maybe . . ."

Charlotte shook her head and brushed a strand of Emily's blonde hair back from her face. "Oh, Emily. I can't fix things for you. As much as I love Ashley and Hunter, they are *your* friends, and—"

"And I need to make things right?" Emily mumbled.

Charlotte squeezed her shoulder. "Yes, you need to make things right. And while I commend you for trying to reach out to Nicole, I'm sorry that so many other things went wrong."

"Yeah, I wish I could go back and do it over. I would rather have gone to the barrel races and had Ashley spend the night."

"Well, it's not too late to create new memories. The fair isn't over. Summer isn't over. Why don't you think about what you can do to show Ashley and Hunter how much you care?" Charlotte tucked her hair behind her ear. "And

I want you to know something else too." She paused, trying to figure out how to say what she wanted to say. "You reached out to Nicole. You did what was right. You forgave her for her words at the fair, and you tried again. And even though things didn't work out the way you wanted them to, I'm sure God is smiling down at you because you chose to love someone who is very difficult to love."

Charlotte looked at her watch and noticed she was late. "And when I get back tonight you can tell me about what your plan is to make things right with Ashley and Hunter. Deal?"

"Yeah, okay." Emily smiled. "Deal."

Charlotte turned to leave and then paused. She glanced back over her shoulder. "Remember, Emily. You messed up, but they are your friends. They will still love you."

Emily nodded, and Charlotte could see tears springing to her granddaughter's eyes. Then she turned and left, knowing, trusting, that Emily could take it from here.

Chapter
Twenty-Two

The scents assaulted Charlotte again as she entered the fairgrounds, and even though they worked with animals on the farm, the fair had certain smells all its own.

For one, each livestock barn smelled differently—and the smells often became overpowering when that many animals of similar type congregated together.

She passed the swine barn, noticing the ammonia scent. Passing the cattle and sheep barns, the fragrance of sweet sawdust was even more overpowering than the animals. But the most intriguing smells came once she got past the barns and moved to the row of food booths—Lions Club, Rotary, the high school cheerleaders.

Charlotte hurried to the pie booth, knocking on the back door to be let in. Rosemary opened the door and stood in the doorway, not letting her through.

"What are you doing here?" Rosemary asked with mock sternness. Yet she couldn't hold the frown for long and broke into a smile.

"I came to work, cut pies maybe. Just as long as I don't have to make change. It's been a busy week, and my mind feels like mush."

"No, I didn't make myself clear. You're not supposed to be working today. A few of us added an hour to our shifts to cover yours."

"Are you serious? Why?"

"I left a message with Bob. Didn't you get it?"

Charlotte shook her head. "No, but he has been a little busy. Last time I saw him he was helping one of the cameramen hook a camera up to his tractor so they could film the ground from the tractor's point of view, although he wasn't too happy about it."

Rosemary laughed. "Well, that sounds, uh, interesting, but I can't believe he didn't tell you. Would have saved you a trip."

"Well, I don't mind. Thank you for doing that. Maybe I'll just walk around and check out some of my exhibits. Would you believe, I haven't even checked on my entries yet."

Rosemary shooed Charlotte along, and she wandered back to the homemakers building. Charlotte had spent so much time within these walls that walking in almost seemed like returning home.

She loved seeing the bright colors of the canned fruits and the pies baked to perfection with artistic designs cut in the tops for steam release.

There were all kinds of pies displayed on tables with risers so those near the back could be seen.

Charlotte took her time and didn't hurry to the end to see how her pie had placed.

She knew all the ins and outs of pie baking. The rumor was that cherry pies always showed better and placed higher because the bright redness looked so nice through the flaky lattice crusts. Knowing this, Charlotte purposely didn't enter cherry pies at the fair. It was almost her way of proving that idea to be false, and over the years she'd won with everything from apple, to blackberry, to lemon meringue.

She paused for a minute to look at the brownies because many of her friends enjoyed entering that division. Glancing down at the dried-up dark chocolate bars, she wondered how some of them had won a prize. It just made her realize how many days had passed. Having done this for so long, she knew that three days earlier they'd been elegant displays of dark, moist chocolate, chopped walnuts, and light dustings of powdered sugar.

Charlotte finally reached the end of the row where her pie sat. Her throat tightened and her heart fell when she noticed a red ribbon on her apple-caramel. She looked closer, unsure if she was seeing that correctly. Charlotte felt foolish, but she couldn't remember ever receiving a red ribbon in any category before. A new sympathy for Christopher washed over her.

She saw other people walking down the line, viewing the pies, and she moved on. She'd entered pies enough times to know they were judged on texture, taste, and appearance. Where had she gone wrong? She shuffled on, moving to the next aisle.

In the past she'd always admired the handmade crochet items—mostly pastel yarn that was crafted into doilies, afghans, and sweaters—but today her eyes barely skimmed them. How could she have gone wrong?

Charlotte moved to the quilts next and wasn't surprised

to see that Rosemary had again won best of show. *At least two of my family members succeeded.*

Charlotte dutifully moved from one exhibition to the next, letting her eyes scan the produce: the apples, various squash and pumpkins, and all the potatoes—the big bakers, the red new potatoes, and even the yams and sweet potatoes. She tried to act interested, but instead her mind turned to the pie booth and she suddenly felt horrified that she'd attempted to replace all the pies that had been smashed.

What was I thinking? I'm a red-ribbon winner.

"How are you doing, Charlotte?" A voice interrupted Charlotte's thoughts, and she turned to see the high school receptionist, Margo Needleman, standing there.

Margo patted her strawberry blonde hair and then gave Charlotte a quick hug.

"I'm doing well. Are you ready for school?" Charlotte forced a smile.

Margo had been the receptionist for a dozen years, at least, and was the go-to person for anything at the high school.

Margo chuckled. "I'm never ready for summer's end, but at the same time I'm looking forward to seeing all the kids. They always change so much over the summer—especially the boys. And what about you?" Margo asked. "Are you having a good day?"

"I'll be doing better after I have a little snack." Charlotte patted her stomach. "I've been promising myself a funnel cake all week, and I haven't had any yet."

"Those things are addictive, aren't they?" Margo chuckled.

"I told myself not to eat more than one or two a day this year. Both my bank account and my waistband will thank me for it."

Margo just stood there, smiling, and Charlotte had a feeling there was something the woman wasn't saying.

"So, I heard a rumor that Pete is going to be the new hunk in Shae Lynne's music video. I've heard that his girl-friend Dana Simons is quite upset about it."

Charlotte laughed. "Well that's a very false rumor. Pete does have a part, but I think it's farmer number two. Bob is farmer number one." She smiled. "I can assure you, there is a very hunky hunk on the farm, and playing that part would be the last thing Pete would do."

"Are you sure?" Margo cocked an eyebrow. "I heard it from Dana's mother herself."

Charlotte was about to refute the idea again when she felt a tap on her shoulder.

"Hi, Charlotte. I was hoping to catch up with you. Do you have a few minutes to talk?" She glanced up into the face of Misty Roberts, one of the reporters at the *Bedford Leader*.

"Uh, I guess so." Charlotte turned to Margo. "Can we finish this later?"

Margo seemed reluctant to go, but she took the clue. "Yes, uh, of course. Maybe we can catch up over mini-doughnuts sometime."

Charlotte turned back to Misty. "Thanks. You just saved me from a very awkward situation. How can I help you?"

"Well, I wanted to do a story . . ."

Charlotte held up her hand, stopping the woman's words. "I'm not the one you need to talk to. If you go to the office, you can talk to Hannah or Betty. They're the ones in charge of all the PR stuff for the fair. Or, I have Hannah's cell phone number if you'd like it." Charlotte dug into her purse, looking for a piece of paper.

"Oh, no. I didn't want to talk about the fair. I wanted to interview you about the video. I was just out at the farm and interviewed Shae Lynne, but wanted to get a comment from you before I turn in my story. I'm right up against my deadline."

"I don't really have much to say except that we're honored that we were given this opportunity, and we hope it will benefit the fair as well." Charlotte hoped her voice didn't sound too firm. "Speaking of which, shouldn't the fair get top billing?"

Other people stood at a distance, close enough to listen in on the conversation but not too close that it seemed they were eavesdropping.

An uneasiness crawled over Charlotte like a dozen of those daddy longlegs spiders that Christopher liked catching.

Misty readjusted her camera bag on her shoulder and didn't seem hindered. "Yes, well, this story does have to do with the fair. After all, Shae Lynne is being touted as the grand finale."

"That's true, but I just don't want to step on anyone's toes."

"Oh, everyone will be just fine. Thanks for your comments. Now I've got to interview the lady who won the best of show in the pie division. They're a new family in town, and the woman's son Hunter won in the barrel races. I thought it would be nice to spotlight the family."

"Chloe Norris." Charlotte mumbled.

"Yes, that's her. I forgot she's your neighbor," Misty said.

"They bought the old Schnurnberger place. Yes, Hunter is a very nice boy."

Charlotte glanced at the pies again, focusing in on the one with the purple best-of-show ribbon. "She sure does make a pretty pie."

"Oh, and so tasty too. She brought one down to our office," Misty exclaimed before remembering who she was talking to. She cleared her throat. "I'm sure the judges had a tough, tough choice picking best of show; that's for sure. You always make great pies too. I requested a slice of yours from the Amen Pies booth. I hope you're not too upset."

"Upset? Why would I be upset?" Charlotte patted her cheek. "No, I'm just tired, that's all. This is what the fair is about, friendly competition. We all encourage each other, learn from each other."

"Oh yes. Well, here comes Chloe now."

Charlotte turned and noticed Hunter's mom approaching. She was tall and thin and looked far too young to have a son Hunter's age. *She looks great in blue jeans, has a smile that lights up a room, and can bake an award-winning pie too.* Charlotte forced a smile.

"Misty, are you ready for the interview?" Chloe asked.

"Yes, ma'am. Just finishing up with Charlotte here."

"Hello, Charlotte." Chloe's eyes were warm and friendly.

"Congratulations on your big win," Charlotte offered, with what she hoped sounded like sincerity.

"Thank you. You know, I almost didn't enter the pie competition because I'd heard you were impossible to beat."

Charlotte attempted to chuckle. "We can see that's not true. Your pie is beautiful, and I've heard quite tasty too."

"Why, thank you. Maybe I should drop one by tomorrow. I'm sure Shae Lynne would love a pie."

"Yes," Charlotte nodded. "I'm sure she would. Speaking of which, I better get home. I left Bob to oversee things, and I want to make sure he's not too frazzled." Even as Charlotte said the words she remembered the fair board meeting. *Would it be so bad to miss it just this once?*

"Great. Well then, tell Shae Lynne to expect a pie from me." Chloe's singsong voice followed Charlotte out the door.

Charlotte nodded and hurried out of the building. One day people were upset because of her connection to the singer, and the next minute Charlotte felt like the most popular girl in school. Charlotte didn't know which was worse.

She hurried over to the staff parking lot where she'd parked and climbed into her car. *Quiet and peace, at last.* Yet even as she watched the fairgrounds growing smaller in her rearview mirror, she couldn't leave the heavy feeling behind.

A red ribbon.

Charlotte certainly wasn't up to her usual standard. Mixed with her disappointment was an uneasy feeling that she shouldn't be so upset about something so silly.

But even as she thought that, deep down she knew it was more than that. She'd been going through the week trying to force everything into the box it had always fit in before. The hardest part was not being able to accept the week for what it was. Accept the changes for what they were.

Life changes. Expectations are dashed. Lord, help me to be okay with whatever you bring to my path. After all, if it's here, it's from you. Help me to remember that.

Chapter
Twenty-Three

Charlotte arrived home to find Pete on the front porch swing with his arm around Shae Lynne. A small group of people were circled around them including the lighting guys, the producers, and the cameramen. Pete and Shae Lynne were laughing and smiling at each other, and instantly Charlotte's stomach fell.

"Isn't it cool?" Sam hurried to her as soon as she climbed from the car.

"Isn't what cool?" Charlotte asked, narrowing her gaze at the singer and her son.

"Shae Lynne said the other guy they brought in looked like a Vegas bar dancer, not a Nebraska farmer. She asked Pete to be the main lead, and he agreed."

"He did?" Charlotte paused mid-step. "And why on earth did he do that?"

Sam shrugged. "I don't know. He wouldn't say. He just told me he had a surprise for Dana, and it was worth acting like a dope for a few hours."

Charlotte nodded and then quietly approached Bob, who was leaning against the fence post, watching. She approached and motioned for him to lean down so she could whisper in his ear.

"Does Dana know?" Charlotte whispered.

Bob's eyes were focused on the scene on the porch, and he didn't seem to pay attention to her question.

Charlotte motioned for him to lean down again. "Do you think Pete's going to use the money for an engagement ring?" She whispered louder.

Bob shrugged and placed a finger over her mouth, shushing her. Charlotte could take a hint. She pressed her lips together and watched as Pete stood, stretched out his hand, and pulled Shae Lynne up from the swing. Then he drew her into his arms, and they began to dance to a song playing in the background, sung by Shae Lynne.

If Charlotte wasn't here, seeing it with her own eyes, she would never have believed Pete to be so . . . smooth, care-free, romantic.

"Okay, cut!" Will yelled.

Immediately Pete dropped his hands, releasing Shae Lynne, and stepped back. Then he moved to the front porch steps and sat down with his elbows resting on his knees and his hands on his chin like a nervous schoolboy waiting for his next assignment.

As soon as the director yelled cut, everyone seemed to spring into motion. Hair and makeup people hurried toward Shae Lynne for touch-ups. The lighting guy reset the large light on the stand, and Emily came running toward Charlotte from where she'd been sitting by the tree.

"Grandma, did you hear? Uncle Pete is going to play Shae Lynne's boyfriend in the video." Emily squealed the words with excitement.

"Yes, I heard it at the fair, and now I *see* it." Charlotte placed a hand on her hip and lifted one eyebrow.

"Isn't that the coolest thing ever? I never thought I'd be related to someone famous."

"Yeah, me neither." Charlotte focused her gaze at Pete. He glanced up, caught her eyes, and then quickly looked away.

"Well, I'm heading over to do the evening chores." Bob said, looping his thumbs over the buckles on his overalls. "It's going to take me twice as long though. With Trudy thinking she's a star and all, she's asking for solid-gold hay in her stall." Bob winked at Charlotte.

"Oh yeah, well, I don't think this is very funny. Any of it." Charlotte kept her voice low, but she could tell by Bob's face that he knew she meant business. "I mean, having the video people here is fine. I can deal with the people at the fair talking. I can deal with everyone wanting to stop by the farm to see it for themselves. That doesn't bother me. But has anyone asked what Dana thinks about all this?"

"We know what Dana thinks." Bob placed a hand on Charlotte's arm.

Charlotte glanced up, surprised.

"She was here earlier. She didn't want to stay around and watch—mostly for Pete's sake. She thought he'd have a hard time acting with her around, but they talked about it, and she said she was okay with the idea."

Charlotte swatted his arm. "I asked you that earlier, Bob. You could have said something instead of having me stand here and seethe."

"You asked that?"

"Yes, when I first walked up. Oh, never mind. I just feel bad, thinking about poor Dana, wondering how she feels about other people moving in . . . ."

Charlotte felt tears pooling in her eyes, and she quickly blinked them away, wondering what her problem was.

"Why don't you join me in the barn, Char? Maybe Trudy will give you an autograph," Bob joked, but his tone was gentle. He waved Emily away, and their granddaughter got the hint and headed back to her spot near the tree.

Bob wrapped an arm around Charlotte's shoulders. He pulled her close as they walked. "So you want to tell me about it?"

Charlotte shook her head. "Not really."

"Is it the video crew that's bothering you? There are a lot of people here."

"No."

"The fair board?"

She shrugged. "Not really."

"The fact that Pete's dancing with some girl other than the one you envisioned him marrying and settling down with?"

"I guess not. I mean, it's just acting."

"Okay." Bob paused at the entrance to the barn. "What is it?"

Charlotte felt her chin tremble. "I got a red ribbon on one of my pies."

Bob tried to hide the small smile, but Charlotte wasn't fooled.

"I know. I'm just being silly. I'm an old fool."

Bob shrugged. "Should I repeat what I believe you told Christopher . . . that the whole point of the competition is cheering each other on and doing one's best?"

"You don't have to remind me."

"Well, good." Bob lifted her chin and kissed her forehead. "Now, woman, get inside and make me some dinner, and if you'd like, I'll give you a blue ribbon. Heck, I'll even borrow Christopher's crayons and color one myself."

Charlotte smiled and then headed toward the house, but as she hurried up the porch steps even the idea of Bob coloring a blue ribbon for her didn't make her feel better. She remembered that there was another fair board meeting in the morning and the special fair edition of the *Bedford Leader* would be out as well, reporting all the winners. The fact was that the drama of the fair wasn't over.

In fact, it might just be gearing up.

EMILY LEANED HER BACK against the porch and took another large bite from the peanut butter and jelly sandwich. Just after Grandma had gotten home, Will had surprised everyone with another catered meal from Mel's Place. Everyone except Emily was excited about the ribs, but she didn't want to make a scene. So instead she slipped inside and made her own sandwich, and now she was settling down to watch the filming again.

The producers wanted to film the same scene they'd done earlier, only this time they wanted to film it in the twilight of the evening. Lights shone on the porch, but the rest of the farm was dark. Only the fading sun on the western horizon cast a faint glow.

"Hey there."

Emily heard a soft whisper just behind the tree. Her heart jumped to her throat, and she let out a little squeal.

"Shh," the voice said. A shadowy figure walked around the tree and sat down beside Emily. She placed a hand over her pounding chest and then she let out a long, low breath when she realized it was Miss Simons.

"What are you doing, trying to kill me with fright?" Emily whispered.

"Shhh, I don't want Pete to know I'm here."

Miss Simons buttoned up her sweater.

"Where did you park?" Emily looked over her shoulder at the gravel road.

Miss Simons leaned close to Emily, whispering in her ear. "Way down at Hannah's house. Then I walked down."

Emily's gaze searched the woman's face in the dim light and noticed her frown. "I thought you didn't want to watch."

"I don't, not really. But I couldn't stay away either." Miss Simons shrugged. "I thought it might be a good idea to get a peek of it now. You know, before millions of viewers watch it on CMT."

"Yeah, well, I'm not sure that's a great idea."

"Okay, action!" Will called again.

As they watched, Pete reached out his hand toward Shae Lynne and guided her off the porch swing. Then, with a laugh, he picked her up and swung her around, nestling his face close to her neck.

"Ugh." Dana let out a low moan. "I think I'm going to throw up."

Emily looked over and noticed Miss Simons covering her face with her hands. "Miss Simons, it's just acting. You should see him after each scene cut. He looks like a lost puppy. Maybe this isn't a good idea. Why don't I walk back to Hannah's with you?"

Dana stood, wiping her palms on her jeans. She didn't answer, but she nodded.

They silently, secretly moved from the lawn to the gravel road, walking in the ditch so as not to be seen.

As soon as they were a distance away, Dana kicked up a huge cloud of dust with her tennis shoe. "I can't believe Pete agreed to this. I can't believe I said it was okay."

Emily thought about reminding her again it was just acting, but she knew better then to say anything. Growing up, it was a lesson she'd learned from her mom. Better to hold your tongue than say the wrong thing at the wrong time.

"I don't understand. Did you see the way Pete looked at her? He doesn't even look at me that way."

"Well, think of it this way." Emily tried to sound upbeat. "In a few days, that woman will be gone—completely out of the picture. And then you'll have Pete all to yourself again."

Miss Simons didn't comment, so Emily continued on. "Yeah, in a few weeks school will start. We'll all get back into our normal routine."

They continued on, nearing Hannah's house, but Dana still didn't answer. Emily's heart felt heavy, picturing Miss Simons going home alone, thinking about Pete and Shae Lynne.

"Hey." Emily placed a hand on Miss Simons's arm. "I think there's something you should know . . . about the video and all that stuff."

Miss Simons paused and wiped her cheek. For the first time, Emily realized she was crying. Emily also realized she too was starting to get mad at Pete for doing what he did.

"I'm not supposed to say anything, but I heard Pete telling someone that he was doing the video for you."

"For me? Ha!" A disbelieving laugh burst from Miss Simons's lips.

"No, seriously. He said he didn't mind being a dork for a few hours because it paid well and that meant he could do something nice for you."

Dana stood there, studying Emily's face as if trying to decide if she could believe her or not.

"Are you s-serious?" she finally sputtered.

"Yup." Emily placed a finger to her lips. "But don't tell anyone. Uncle Pete would kill me if he knew I told you."

Dana nodded and turned, and then she continued on to Hannah's with lighter steps.

When she'd almost reached her car, she paused. "Emily, what do you think it is? Do you have any clue what the surprise is?"

Emily shrugged. "Well, Uncle Pete didn't give any hints." She looked at Miss Simons's left hand. "But I think I have an idea."

Dana nodded and pressed her lips together. "Yeah, well, maybe we shouldn't guess. I don't want to jinx the, his, uh, surprise or anything."

"Good idea." Emily twisted her fingers near her lips as if she were locking it up with a key. "The secret, whatever it is, is safe with me."

Chapter
Twenty-Four

F ront page!"
Dwayne Cook pushed the small red and white cardboard boat away from him. A minute ago it had been filled with hash browns, but now only a glob of ketchup and a few overcooked potato shreds remained.

"Do you think that's right?" He flashed the newspaper for all the other board members to see. "I'm sure as responsible members of the fair board the Stevensons would have declined letting the reporter onto their farm."

Charlotte had awakened early and had hurried to get breakfast on the table before heading into the fair board meeting with Bob. The video shoot had run late last night, and now her eyelids felt like sandpaper. The last thing she needed was for Dwayne to make a big deal about the newspaper story that had shown up under today's headline.

Charlotte took a sip of her coffee, and tried to think of the right way to respond. Even without looking at him, Charlotte knew Bob was about to explode. His hand that rested on the wooden table was curled into a tight ball. She set down her coffee and placed her hand over his, patting it.

"The concert is part of the fair, not the other way around," Dwayne continued.

"I don't see why we allowed the video shoot to be on the Stevensons' farm in the first place," Betty butted in. "Just a few months ago they got that award . . . what was it for?"

"Adams County Farm of the Year." Hannah jutted out her chin. "And I think it was well deserved."

"Yes, that's it. Adams County Farm of the Year," Betty continued, ignoring Hannah's glare. She patted her white hair and softened her tone, peering at Charlotte like a kindergarten teacher who just wants her student to obey. "I mean, I was fine with *that* award because I knew the family could probably use some good news after all the difficulties of the past year, but there are other farms in the area that are struggling. Those people could use some publicity too."

Charlotte opened her mouth, preparing to again explain that she and Bob hadn't sought out the producers. But before she could get one word out, the conversation exploded again.

"And now they have the front page too?" Dwayne patted the paper. "I think the Stevensons are a great family, but enough is enough."

"Grandma?" Charlotte felt a tug on her arm and turned, noticing Emily standing there. Emily and Christopher had ridden in with Charlotte to watch the 4-H showmanship events that some of their friends were involved in. After the morning events, Christopher was going to spend the rest of the day hanging out around the fair with Dylan. And Emily, she hoped, was going to make amends with her friends.

"Grandma is everything alright?" Emily asked and Charlotte could tell from the look on her face that she'd heard more than she should have. Emily had enough to be concerned about with Nicole's ugly comments. She didn't need to worry about adult problems.

"Everything's fine, dear. What do you need?"

"Grandma, you were supposed to meet me over at the arts and crafts barn," Emily whispered. "The lady from the newspaper wants to get a photo of me with my best of show ribbon. I've been waiting."

"Oh, Emily, you're right." Charlotte glanced at her watch, shocked by how long they'd been sitting there discussing things that should be non-issues to the fair board. "I'm so sorry, I completely forgot."

Charlotte rose, attempting to ignore the conversation.

She patted Hannah on the arm. "I'm not sure what they'll decide, but just give me a call later."

Hannah nodded and gave Charlotte a sympathetic smile.

"Bob, are you coming?" Charlotte leaned down and whispered in his ear.

"No, Charlotte. I'm going to see this out. This is our reputation they're talking about. How I see it, news is news, and I don't need anyone's permission before I talk to anyone about what's happening on our farm." Bob jutted out his chin.

Charlotte nodded and led Emily out of the building.

"So they're upset about the video?" Emily finally asked just before they got to the arts and crafts building.

"I wouldn't say *upset*." Charlotte placed an arm around

her granddaughter's shoulders. "This is a stressful time for a lot of people, and the video just put another kink in their knotted neck muscles. Just ignore it."

"Yeah, I'm trying to, but it seems like everyone's talking about it. When I was in the exhibit building, waiting for you, I heard two women talking about Shae Lynne. They were saying that she's dating Uncle Pete. I thought I should set them straight, but then I remembered how you and Grandpa always tell me to respect my elders."

"That's right, Emily. I'm proud of you. And for the most part, I'm just trying to refute anything that's adding fuel to the fiery rumors. And . . ." Charlotte sighed. "I just look at it this way. A week from now the fair will be over, the video will be done, Shae Lynne will be at a different fair, and we'll still be a part of this community. There's no need to argue or fuss. And in a month those who are blabbing the loudest now will have forgotten what got them so riled up."

Charlotte slowed her footsteps as they entered the building. Sure enough, Misty was there waiting for them. "Now, go ahead and give her your best smile," Charlotte told Emily. "Let's not let anything take away from this moment."

Charlotte watched as Misty snapped photos of Emily, thankful that her granddaughter was getting the attention. As she stood in the doorway she felt someone brush against her and was surprised to find Sam, Jordan, Arielle, Natalie, and another young woman standing there.

"You guys are up early. Are you taking a break from the video shoot?" Charlotte glanced at the faces of the teens.

"Actually, I've talked my new cousin, *Trudy*, into coming to the fair and hanging out with us for a while."

Charlotte glanced past Natalie to the petite blonde who was standing right beside her. "*Shae Lynne*?" Charlotte mouthed.

Shae Lynne was dressed in one of Emily's T-shirts and a simple pair of jeans. She slipped an old pair of sunglasses down her nose and smiled at Charlotte. "Well, I take that as a good sign that it took you a while to figure out it was me. You know, Jordan had a good idea. I don't get time for myself to just hang out. They convinced me I could be an added cousin, and no one would be the wiser. Although I'm not sure how I feel about being named after a cow." She glared at Sam.

"So, I take it you're done with the video shoot?"

"Yeah, for the most part. I think they're getting some final shots today. Thankfully we found a body double to fill in for the long kiss at the end."

"The kiss?"

"You know, Grandma." Sam nudged Charlotte with his elbow. "Every good country video needs to end with a kiss."

"Who did you find?" Charlotte's eyes widened as she imagined Pete's opinion about having to kiss a stranger.

Shae Lynne leaned close to Charlotte's ear. "Well, with a long, blonde wig and the magic of splicing scenes together, Dana was the perfect fit. I hope Pete doesn't mind having to kiss her at least fifty times—you know how Will is about getting the perfect shot."

Charlotte laughed and then covered her mouth when Misty looked in their direction.

"Okay, run along now. Have fun at the fair and don't get sick on too much junk food."

"Are you kidding?" Shae Lynne pushed her sunglasses back up her nose. "I can't wait to eat a corn dog and then get on the Squirrel Cages. I bet Jordan I can do it without puking." Then, with laughter, the teens and Shae Lynne strolled toward the carnival rides.

"I suppose, if anything, this is a vacation Jordan will never forget," Charlotte mumbled to herself.

Chapter Twenty-Five

S am couldn't help but laugh at the dumb look on Jordan's face. Even if people didn't recognize Shae Lynne without her fancy hair and sparkly clothes, they should have figured something was up by the way Jordan strutted around with a huge smile, talking nonstop to "Trudy." He was wondering if he might need to rescue her from Jordan's crush.

After eating a corn dog and hitting the rides, they decided to slow things down by walking through the animal barns. Sam had to admit it was kind of cute seeing the little kids with determined looks on their faces using shovels and big push brooms twice their size to clean up the stalls.

On most of the stalls there were large, colorful posters telling about the kids and their animals. Shae Lynne stopped to read one written by a little girl about her lamb Marshmallow.

"I can't believe they are actually able to raise these animals and sell them to market. I'm too much of a sissy. I think I'd cave, buy it back and take it on my bus." Shae Lynne glanced around. "I mean, I'd take it home and keep it forever." She chuckled.

"Yeah, well, that's just the life of a farmer." Sam straightened his shoulders, caught a little off guard that he actually meant what he said.

They walked around for a while and the more they walked the quieter Shae Lynne became. As they walked through the arts and crafts building, Shae Lynne started humming a catchy tune and then added some words:

"Ferris wheels that smell like grease. That hawker's smile captivates, just like the men Mama told me to stay away from . . ." Shae Lynne hummed some more then softly sang, "The Tilt-A-Whirl has got me dizzy . . . or maybe it's just the sight of you, baby. All I know is that my mind is spinning, spinning even after the ride has stopped."

Sam and the others circled around and gazed at Shae Lynne, both surprised by the way she was stringing the words together and the distant look in her eyes that told them that while she was still physically at the fair her mind was in another place.

"Hey, Sam." Shae Lynne removed her sunglasses and set them back on top of her head. "Do you know of a place that's kind of quiet where I can write for a while? I have this song idea that's going around in my head, and I have a horrible problem remembering. If I don't get it down on paper right away, I lose it completely."

"Uh, sure. There's a conference area in the back of the fair office. I'm sure if no one's there they wouldn't mind you popping in."

"Really?" Shae Lynne's face brightened, and she patted his arm. "That would be great."

Sam turned to the others. "You guys can go ahead to the Country Kitchen, and I'll meet you there."

Jordan seemed slightly disappointed, but Sam wasn't too worried about that. What he was concerned about was getting Shae Lynne to the office before she got completely lost in her thoughts.

He led her to the office, and Hannah seemed tickled pink to set Shae Lynne up in the back with paper and pen and a promise not to let anyone bother her while she worked.

Sam hung by the door a few minutes, watching and listening. Partly because she didn't tell him to leave but mostly because he'd never seen words come so fast to anyone.

"Signs painted, some faded," he heard Shae Lynne sing under her breath. "Snow cones, hot dogs, lemonade. It's not about the bright lights to me, it's my home, my community. The end of summer. A celebration. Our way of life that's uncomplicated. Sunflowers planted by the front gate that welcome guests with a serenade. Shooting games, throwing darts. The stuffed dog my daddy won—it hit the mark, of my heart."

"The Tilt-O-Whirl has got me dizzy," she repeated. "Or maybe it's the sight of you, baby. All I know is that my mind is spinning, spinning even after the ride has stopped."

LATER THAT EVENING, Emily blew out a big breath as she waited outside Mel's Place. She had arranged for Hunter and Ashley to meet her at the diner at eight o'clock sharp. She glanced through the window and saw that they were chatting by the register as Ashley was cashing out.

Her grandmother's words replayed in her mind.

Remember, Emily, you messed up, but they are your friends. They will still love you.

Emily pushed the door open and hurried toward Ashley and Hunter before she lost her nerve.

"Okay, this is how it is. I blew it, big time." She turned to Hunter, looking up into his blue eyes. "I totally failed you as a friend by missing a very important event." Then she turned to Ashley. "And I messed up by not being there when I said I would, and for making other plans, stupid plans." She took a deep breath. "But I will do whatever it takes to make it up to you."

"I'm not sure you *can* make it up to us, Emily," Hunter said. "We were counting on you."

"The worst part of it," Ashley echoed, "is that you totally blew us off and got sucked in by people who were only using you to get to Shae Lynne."

"I realize that now," Emily said. "In fact, I think I realized it then, but I just didn't know how to get out of the situation. My grandma had asked me to try to be nice to Nicole, and I thought I was doing the right thing."

Ashley and Hunter stood with their arms crossed and listened to Emily's feeble attempt at explaining herself.

Emily went on, "Really, you guys. You have to know that I had a miserable time, and I know I hurt your feelings, and I hope you can forgive me."

Ashley's face softened a bit, and she moved toward Emily. "Listen. Maybe you can't exactly make it up to us, but we are your friends, and we do forgive you."

"You do?" Emily asked with a little relief—as well as wonder.

"Yes, we do," Hunter agreed. "But don't let it happen again."

"You can count on me from now on," Emily said and gave each of her friends a big hug.

Ashley punched her arm. "I'm glad that's over and we're friends again. And since we're here, and we're all free, I think we should head to the fair."

"For rides." Hunter punched the air.

"And games," Ashley commented.

"And food . . ." Emily started and then changed her mind. "Or we can just get something here," she said, eyeing the cinnamon rolls in the glass case.

"Yeah, sure, my mom won't mind," Ashley walked around to the back of the case. "I love to share, but only with my bestest, bestest friends."

CHARLOTTE SLIPPED HER HAND into Bob's, thankful for a few minutes to spend time together during this busy week.

"Strange how we're surrounded by people in this overflowing fairground and it's the first minute of peace we've had all week." Charlotte chuckled.

"Well, I'm glad I was able to sneak you away. With the concert tomorrow night, I figured this is our only opportunity to walk around the fair," Bob replied.

Charlotte squeezed his hand. "So how should we celebrate? With a funnel cake? A walk around the exhibition hall to pick up our free balloons and rulers, or—"

"How about a twirl on the Ferris wheel?" Bob interrupted.

Charlotte smiled. "You took the words right out of my mouth."

They walked to the line and noticed it was long, yet Charlotte didn't seem to mind. "Can you believe the video is done? I can't wait to see it."

"Well, you're not going to have to wait too long. I talked to Will this morning, and they're going to drop something off before they leave town on Sunday."

"Honestly? They can create it that fast?"

"Well, it will be the unedited version, but Will said it will give us an idea of what the finished product will look like. He also said not to be too disappointed if there are a lot of things they leave out. He says they shoot about fifty times more footage than they'll ever be able to use in a three-minute video."

"Just as long as I get to see that handsome farmer boy." Charlotte smiled. "I never imagined my son would be famous."

The line moved along, and soon Bob and Charlotte were climbing onto the ride.

"Buckle up," the Ferris wheel operator said as they climbed in.

"Seat belts?" Charlotte smiled as she snapped the belt around her waist. "You'd think they'd have thought of this sooner, wouldn't you, Bob? Remember when we'd bring the kids on the Ferris wheel when they were little?"

"Of course I remember. How could I forget? Pete would rock the seat and scare Bill."

"Yes, and while you were riding with the boys I'd spend the whole time trying to get Denise to keep her rear on the seat and not lean over the bar. She was always so social, calling and waving to everyone she knew."

They were quiet for a while, each lost in thought as the Ferris wheel moved one seat at a time, loading and unloading. As the ride started, Charlotte rested her head on Bob's shoulder. She let out a contented sigh as she marveled at the lights of the fair below them.

"You know, I always have a special place in my heart for the fair."

"Really, why?"

"Well, to me, it was like the first phase of our engagement."

Bob removed his ball cap and scratched his head. "Really? Did I forget something? I was there, wasn't I?" He laughed.

Charlotte softly elbowed his ribs. "No, it wasn't you. It was my other husband."

Bob returned his hat and nodded. "Just checking."

"No, seriously, remember you were working as a maintenance worker for the fair, and you had me out here with you doing everything from setup to takedown."

"Yeah, I remember that. I remember being impressed that such a cute little thing could haul around those big tables."

"Amazing what one will do to get the attention of a guy, isn't it?"

The Ferris wheel started to slow and Charlotte knew the unloading would begin. She glanced around, taking in the view.

"But I don't understand. What did that have to do with our engagement?" Bob said.

"Don't you remember? I was out here working, and

Rosemary showed up. She said I'd better be getting a big diamond for all that work."

"Oh yes, I remember now. Then a few weeks later I remember asking what you thought about her idea of the diamond."

"A few weeks? More like a few months. The waiting was horrible. I never thought you'd propose." She smiled, recalling the long wait.

"I don't remember how much time passed, but I do remember what you said."

"Really?" Charlotte searched her memory, trying to remember. But nothing surfaced.

"Yes, you said, 'Yeah, I think the diamond should be huge.'" Bob laughed.

Charlotte joined in. "You know I was joking, right?"

"Yes." Bob lifted her hand with her simple wedding band. "Or at least I sure hope you were."

"I got *you*, and that's what I wanted out of the deal." Charlotte leaned up, rocking the chair slightly and placed a quick peck on Bob's cheek. "My diamond in the rough."

"Speaking of diamonds," Charlotte commented as Bob held her hand and helped her off the Ferris wheel, "do you think that's what Pete's going to do with the money from the video?"

"Charlotte . . ." Bob's voice mocked sternness. "You know that's none of our business."

"Of course it's not, but I still like to wonder."

Bob pressed his hand to the small of her back as he guided her to the game area. "Yes, well, I guess time will tell." He paused in front of the balloon darts, as if hoping to distract her. "Now, how about I win you a stuffed dog? I'm feeling lucky tonight."

CHARLOTTE HUGGED THE LARGE green-and-white dinosaur to her chest as they headed out of the fair for the night. She'd stopped counting after twenty dollars, knowing that Bob could have bought her a fancy stuffed animal for less. *But it's the thought that counts*, she reminded herself. *I'll treasure it forever*.

They were almost out of the game area when Bob placed a hand on Charlotte's shoulder, stopping her. He pointed ahead and then leaned down to whisper in her ear. "Would you look at that?"

Bob pointed to Sam and Jordan, up ahead. They were attempting to pitch softballs into large milk jugs. Jordan was dressed in Levi's and a cowboy hat. He whooped and hollered when Sam got one in.

Charlotte leaned back against Bob, and he wrapped his arms around her. "It's been good for Jordan to come. Even if we hadn't had the video thing on the farm, I think this week would've been good for him. I think he'll return home with a whole new perspective."

"Yeah, just like it's been good for Sam. He's gotten into trouble, but he's learned a lot too. I think he's turning out to be a different kid than he would have if he'd grown up in San Diego," she answered.

Bob nodded and released his arms. He took Charlotte's hand and led her to the staff parking lot, where his truck waited. He was quiet as they walked, and Charlotte knew his mind was busy thinking about something.

Bob opened the door for her and paused.

"You know, I've been thinking. What if we do donate some of that money we got to the fair?"

Charlotte slid into the seat, allowed him to shut the door, and waited until he got in himself. "Are you feeling guilty? Is all their whining getting to you?"

"No, it was watching Jordan and Sam, actually. What if we donate a little money to start a special fair fund and then encourage others from the community to pitch in too? We could start a scholarship so that a few city kids could come spend a week in the summer at local farms and at the fair."

"*Hmm.* That's certainly something to think about."

It was a quiet ride home. Charlotte let her mind replay all the pros and cons of Bob's suggestion and finally answered as the truck neared their farm.

"You know, it is a good idea. It would stop the community's grumbling about all the attention and money we've gotten lately. More than that, it would help a lot of kids. We could have events for them to sign up for, like the pig wrestling, and maybe teach them how to make a pie or can tomatoes."

"Or train a dog," Bob added.

"Or train a dog." Charlotte turned to him and smiled. "I like it, Bob; I really do. Let's talk to the fair board about it at the next meeting."

"So you're going to stay on the fair board?"

"Yes, I think I will. If we can help make the fair easier and better, well, it's worth it—don't you think?"

"Of course, Charlotte. It takes all of us working together to create a fair with flair."

Chapter
Twenty-Six

Charlotte carried her lawn chair as she walked through the gate to the grandstand with the other members of her family. The race track was fenced, and old wooden bleachers circled three sides of the oval. Faded, painted signs highlighting local businesses hung on the fence. Boyton Feed. Tri-State Tractors. Mel's Place. Charlotte smiled wide at the last one.

Horse trailers and pickup trucks were parked on the far side of the track, but today the guests streaming through the gates hadn't come to see a race or a rodeo. Charlotte followed Bob to the grassy area where they'd constructed a stage and where, in thirty minutes, Charlotte would get to watch the concert she'd been waiting for all week.

"Up there, Grandpa?" Christopher pointed. "Can we sit near the very front?"

With Christopher was his best friend Dylan, dark hair ruffled and his eyes wide with excitement. "Yeah, we want to get close to the front, where the music is really loud!"

"If we get too close we're not going to be able to see much, except for her toes," Sam commented.

Emily waved to Ashley, who hurried over to join them.

"Oh, my goodness. This has been the busiest week ever." Ashley exclaimed. "I think I've made over a thousand coffee drinks. Seriously." She brushed her auburn hair back from her face.

Seeing the group coming up toward the front, Buck approached them from backstage. "Hey, guys, glad you could make it. I hope you're not too comfortable because Shae Lynne had us rope off a whole section for you." Buck pointed to an area where folding chairs had been set up; there was even a table covered with snacks plus a large bucket filled with ice and soft drinks.

"Cool!" Sam said.

"I don't know." Charlotte hesitated. "I'd hate for us to get any special treatment. Folks are already talking . . ."

Buck pressed his finger to his ear, and Charlotte could tell he was listening to someone through an earpiece.

Buck lowered his hand and then turned back to Charlotte. "Well, it's there if you need it."

Charlotte set her lawn chair on the ground, trying to ignore the disappointed looks of the kids.

"Can we at least go over there and get some of the drinks?" Jordan asked. "I'm a growing boy."

Charlotte took a deep breath. "Not tonight. Really, I think this spot is fine."

They settled down, and soon every space around them was filled.

"Oh no!" Emily's eyes grew wide. "I told Anna I'd save them a spot."

"Yeah, and I need a place for Dana too. She was finishing

up her shift at the pie booth; then she's hurrying over," Pete added.

Charlotte turned to Bob, gauging his response.

Instead of answering, he looked over at the roped-off section.

"Okay, let's go. It looks like there's more room over there." Charlotte rose and folded up her chair. "And I guess the flip side is that we're opening up all these spaces for other people."

They moved to the roped-off section, and her grandkids had no problem getting comfortable.

"Wow, this is so cool! Look at all the stuff for us!"

"Just like God to provide like this," Bob said. "Just adding to all he's already given us this week."

Charlotte thought about those words. For most of the week she'd thought about what was being taken away from her week—time, rest, peace of mind. But when she thought about it Bob's way, he was right. God had given them a cushion in their savings account, had brought an old friend from far away, and had given them new ones too. And somehow she'd made it through with enough strength for each day, just like he'd promised.

The rest of their family joined the group, and Dana got there just as the concert started. Charlotte found herself on her feet, singing and clapping to songs she didn't know. And then she cheered when Shae Lynne announced she'd be singing "Always and Forever with You" next. It was the song they had been making the video for this week, the song she had heard at least a hundred different times.

"'Always and Forever with You' is one of my favorite

songs on my new album that will be out for Christmas. And I'd like to dedicate this song to a special couple. Dana and Pete, would you stand?"

Shae Lynne pointed to Pete, and his face turned red. "Don't tell me you can't!"

Reluctantly Pete rose to his feet. Then he stretched out his hand and helped Dana from her chair. The grandstands seemed to go wild with cheers. Then, as quickly as they could, they sat down again.

Emily squealed and took a photo of Shae Lynne singing the song. Christopher jumped up and down with excitement, and Dylan joined him. In her mind's eye, Charlotte could see the two young boys as teenagers, getting into their own style music, whatever that might be. But for now they were just two kids excited about being a part of something big. Even Sam and Jordan gave Pete a high-five when the song finished.

Shae Lynne waited for the cheering to die down, and then she spoke into the microphone again.

"You know, I haven't had a place speak to me in a long time. I've been touring in buses and working in studios for too long. Most of my songs on my last album were written by other people. But this place, it got wrapped around my heart and told me its own story. But before I sing the song I wrote, I'd like to read something else I wrote.

"It's a prayer. I've never written a prayer before. In fact, I haven't prayed much over the past few years, but I have to say that's going to change. The prayer I wrote is about this place. But mostly it's about some special people. They didn't preach to me, but I saw the message of God in their lives. And I'm leaving this place wanting more of him because of their example."

Shae Lynne looked down from the stage and blew Charlotte a kiss, and then she took a piece of paper from her back pocket.

"God, here in this place you've brought me to, surrounded by acres of wheat and corn, I felt I could see all the way to heaven. In the wide, clear sky, it was as if I heard the angels whispering in the wind blowing through the fields. God, you led me to an old farmhouse filled with antiques and memories. You brought me to a solid red barn, a beacon of hope that God will provide through another winter.

"In the past week I've wandered through tall maize on a warm summer's day, and I've relaxed on a cozy porch after a hard day's work. Thank you. Thank you, God. For letting me get to know the delightful people who make Bedford home. Thank you for showing me that faith is still something to trust in and family is where to find home. Amen."

The cheers from the grandstand rose again, and Charlotte felt her chest grow warm. A smile filled her face, and she wasn't sure anything could take it away. Then, as Shae Lynne began to sing, her tight-lipped smile gave away to tears.

"Now for the song. It's not as mushy, but it's a song I'm going to dedicate to all the hard workers from the Adams County Fair. And since I just taught it to my band last night, please bear with us."

Shae Lynne started to strum her guitar, and then she stopped. "Oh yes. Maybe I should tell you the name. It's 'Sunflower Serenade.'"

Signs painted, some faded,
Snow cones, hot dogs, and lemonade.
It's not about bright lights to me,
It's about the joy of summer days.

The Tilt-A-Whirl has got me dizzy,
Or maybe it's from seeing you, baby.
All I know is my mind is spinning,
Spinning even when the ride is done.

The end of summer, a celebration.
Our way of life, uncomplicated.
Sunflowers planted by the front gate.
Welcome guests with a serenade of . . .

Shooting games and throwing darts,
The stuffed dog Daddy won,
It hit the mark.
It hit the mark of my heart.

The end of summer, a celebration.
Our way of life, uncomplicated.
Sunflowers planted by the front gate.
Welcome guests with a serenade of . . . you.

Chapter
Twenty-Seven

Charlotte stepped through the doors of the church with the happy knowledge that the fair was officially over. Later today they were to pick up their entries from the fair office, and after that, Charlotte thought a long bath sounded like a great idea.

Tomorrow would be another long day of taking Jordan to the airport, but then they'd be back in the regular summer routine until school started up again. Charlotte scratched her head, trying to remember what she'd spent her days doing before the fair came to town.

Pastor Evans approached Charlotte as soon as she entered the sanctuary.

"Charlotte, there was a very polite man who stopped by just a few minutes ago, hoping to catch you. He said the bus was heading out of town—whatever that meant."

"Was his name Will?" Charlotte glanced at Bob.

"Yes, it was. I tried to talk him into staying, but he said he was due back in Nashville in the morning."

"Too bad we missed him." Bob frowned.

"Well, he did leave this." Pastor Evans pulled out a DVD from the front cover of his Bible.

"Oh good, it's the music video . . ." Charlotte let her voice trail off. "Thank you, Pastor."

They found their normal seats, and Charlotte was thankful to see Pete with Dana at the far end of the row. She wasn't sure what they had planned for their future, but for the present Charlotte liked the effect that girl was having on her son.

"Please turn to page 217 in your hymnals," Barb Gardner, today's song leader, guided the congregation. "And let us join together to sing 'Amazing Grace.'"

Charlotte had barely finished the first line when she recognized a voice. It wasn't overpowering; rather it was soft and sweet. Charlotte knew she'd recognize that voice anywhere. She resisted the urged to turn around and wave at Shae Lynne. Instead, she just said a silent prayer for the singer's journey—for today's trip and for her path to growing closer to God.

They sang another hymn after that, and when the service ended Charlotte turned to discover Shae Lynne was already gone. She had slipped out of the service, but Charlotte knew the young woman would never be far from her heart.

THE CONSENSUS WAS THAT they'd all watch the music video together and then have lunch. Charlotte's stomach growled as Pete put the DVD into the player, and then the room grew silent as they all waited for it to begin.

It started with Shae Lynne singing in front of the barn, looking out into the fields as she sang. Then there was the briefest glimpse of Pete on the tractor.

"Is that all?" Pete complained. "I think I drove back and forth out there for an hour."

"Shhh," Dana swatted his hand. "I'm trying to watch."

Next there was a close-up of Shae Lynne singing on the porch and of her walking through the sunflowers in the garden. Then there was a brief glimpse of the barn and Shae Lynne leading Trudy out to pasture.

"Our cow is famous!" Christopher exclaimed.

Then there was a shot of Toby sitting at Shae Lynne's feet.

"I told her to sit," Christopher said. "Do you see that? See her ears? Toby is waiting for me to call her to come to me."

A burst of laughter escaped from Charlotte's lips. "Well, in my book that's worthy of a best of show right there!"

And then, at the end of the video, there was the briefest scene of Pete pulling Shae Lynne off the porch and dancing with her. As the song faded, the video ended with Pete and Dana's kiss. Given the lighting and the way the video faded away, it was hard to see that it wasn't Shae Lynne he was kissing with such tender passion.

"Ooh, Uncle Pete." Emily waved her hand in front of her face. "Who knew you were such a stud?"

Pete's face was red as he bragged, "Oh, please. That was nothing."

"What's that supposed to mean?" Dana asked.

"Just that I've got a few tricks up my sleeve," Pete answered.

"Yeah, Uncle Pete?" Emily butted in. "Don't you have a surprise for Dana—I mean, Miss Simons?"

"A surprise? Really?" Dana leaned forward in anticipation.

"Well, uh, actually . . ." Pete eyed Emily. "It's not ready

yet, but there's something coming soon. Uh, yeah, thanks a lot, Emily."

Emily covered her mouth.

Pete glanced back at Dana. "I'm sorry. I do have something, but it's not ready yet."

Charlotte thought she saw the slightest hint of disappointment in the young woman's gaze. Then, as everyone watched, she threw her arms around Pete and gave him a huge hug. Charlotte saw Dana whisper something in his ear. She didn't know what it was, but Pete smiled big.

Dana leaned back. "Hey, that was a good video." She motioned to Sam. "Can you play it again?"

Sam pressed PLAY on the DVD, and Charlotte smiled as she watched Pete and Dana settle further into the couch. Then she reached out and motioned for Bob's hand. When he took her small hands into his large rough ones, Charlotte let out a contented sigh.

"Hey, do you think I can get a copy of this to take back to San Diego?" Jordan stood up. "I totally have to show my friends."

"Why, so you can make fun of us Nebraskans?" Sam smirked.

"Are you kidding? Why would I do that?"

Sam cocked one eyebrow, but he kept his lips sealed.

"Yeah, yeah. I know I made fun of stuff when I first got here, but I didn't realize how things were. People are different here, but . . ." Jordan looked around and then sat back down as if he had just realized he was the center of attention.

"I'd like a video to show people, because I don't think

I can explain it all," Jordan finally said. "I mean, I never realized before how much work goes into growing the food I eat. Or how much there is to do in such a small community." He laughed. "I think I'll go home and sleep for a week."

"I don't like the idea of you having to leave," Sam admitted. "I mean, who can I tease about leeches in Heather Creek?"

"There are leeches in Heather Creek?" Emily blurted out.

"He's kidding, right?" Dana commented.

The room filled with laughter, and Jordan laughed the hardest. "Yeah, but I'm not scared of them. After lunch I'll race you down to the creek."

"You're on," Sam grinned. "After all, we have to make your last day here a good one."

"Are you kidding? Every day's been good." Jordan punched Sam's arm.

"I agree," Charlotte echoed. "Even if it doesn't start out that way, just being together, knowing God is taking care of us, makes it so."

Even as she said the words, she realized the truth of them. It was the simple things in life, the unexpected things, that meant the most after all.

Just like Shae Lynne sang.

About the Author

Tricia Goyer is the author of eight novels, six nonfiction books, and one children's book. She was named Mount Hermon Christian Writers Conference Writer of the Year in 2003. In 2005, her book *Life Interrupted* was a finalist for the Gold Medallion and her novel *Night Song* won American Christian Fiction Writers Book of the Year for Long Historical Romance. In 2006, her novel *Dawn of a Thousand Nights* also won Book of the Year for Long Historical. Tricia has written more than three hundred articles for national publications and hundreds of Bible study notes for the *Women of Faith Study Bible*. Tricia lives with her husband and three kids in Montana, where she homeschools, leads children's church, and mentors teenage mothers.

A Note from the Editors

Guideposts, a nonprofit organization, touches millions of lives every day through products and services that inspire, encourage and uplift. Our magazines, books, prayer network and outreach programs help people connect their faith-filled values to their daily lives. To learn more, visit www.guideposts.com/about or www.guidepostsfoundation.org.

F
GOY

5/17/16